THE WAITING GAME

THE WAITING GAME

ALEXANDER FULLERTON

PETER DAVIES : LONDON

Peter Davies Limited
15 Queen Street, Mayfair, London W1X 8BE
LONDON MELBOURNE TORONTO
JOHANNESBURG AUCKLAND

Printed in Great Britain by
REDWOOD BURN LIMITED
Trowbridge & Esher

To JOHN DETTMER

AUTHOR'S NOTE

This is a novel, and none of the characters in it is intended in any way to resemble or represent an actual person, whether living or dead.

In this connexion, however, I must record that I was on board a British submarine which, in the summer of 1943, sailed for northern waters with orders to rescue a certain Norwegian bishop and his family. The operation was unsuccessful, so I never met the bishop, or any member of his family, nor do I even know his name. This incident from the past has served only as the idea behind my story; and any resemblance between any of the characters – whether British or Norwegian, in the submarine or on shore – and real people, is coincidental and would be greatly regretted.

A.F.

I

SHE was long and black, and, in the parts that showed above the water, slim; the casing widened a little where the for'ard hydroplane guards grew up and out like ears, then narrowed sharply to the pointed, preying bow.

But below the waterline she was as round and as fat as a cow in calf, the saddle-tanks thick bulges on her sides; and like a drunken cow she rolled while she staggered up the long, steep slopes of the waves and hung momentarily on their crests before plunging down and burying the whole of her forepart, almost as far as the three-inch gun just below the front of her bridge, under the heavy, heaving sea. Down in that trough between the rollers she'd drag herself clear, and then the waves' tops all round would be higher than the heads of the men in her bridge, grey-green walls flecked with foam, looming and overhanging; as the bow broke free, her stern would go down hard, the screws would bite and thrust and she'd drive, splitting the dark water in a great V of white, up the slope of the next roller as it flung itself, mountainous, against the line of her jolting, battering advance. The top of the wave, breaking, would rush aft along her casing and explode against the gun and against the front of her bridge, flinging up a ton of green water and dropping it on the heads of the watchkeepers, who for their own safety were lashed there with ropes' ends bent around their waists and secured to solid fittings in the bridge.

As she rolled, one side sliding down into the sea and the bridge leaning over until if a man stretched out a hand he could almost touch the water, the other side, rising, shone blackly, the great bulge of the saddle-tanks sleek and gleaming like the flank of some monstrous seal.

It's a long time ago to remember, but that's how she behaved and how the waves treated her and looked to the men in her bridge. (Today she no longer exists, except perhaps in other forms; they took her apart, when the war was over, for the value of her steel and because she had served her purpose.)

But she was a ship, then: a submarine: and that's how she looked and felt to the men in her bridge as she hammered in towards the grey, windlashed harbour of Lerwick, in the Shetlands, just about dawn on a morning nearly twenty years ago.

2

THE noise of the alarm clock was sudden, splitting; it left you no head, only an empty skull with apertures for ears and that harsh screech boring its way through, a vicious intruder in the night. Only it wasn't night; when he'd stopped the noise and as he lay back on the pillow to collect his wits, he saw grey dawn gathering in the window at the end of the hut. Thoughts and questions became coherent as he watched it, remembering where he was, why – and no answer to that! – and for what reason he'd planned to wake himself at an hour when the world, and he with it, should be asleep.

His name was Lief Olsen, Sub-Lieutenant in the Royal Norwegian Navy, and he was in a Nissen hut in the submarine base on the island of Lerwick. But as to *why* he was here – the question angered him, now, as much as puzzled. He'd asked, where he could, and nobody would tell him; not in Plymouth, not in London, certainly not here. What disturbed him most was a growing conviction that nobody knew. It could happen, that sort of thing, in his own Navy, and no doubt in this British one, to which he was seconded, the secondment reading 'For duty in submarines'. He'd wanted that, asked for it. They'd sent him to the training base at Blyth, in Northumberland, and he'd passed the course, with reasonably high marks; from there, three months ago, he'd been appointed to a new 'V' Class submarine which had been preparing to leave for the Mediterranean. To be exact, for Malta. This suited him very well: the Malta flotilla had higher losses than most, but their patrols were eventful and they had plenty of targets. Better than the long cold emptiness of the North Sea, or the super-heated boredom of the Far East. Olsen knew the world, or much of it; he'd a Second Mate's ticket in a Scandinavian tanker fleet, when the war started, and he'd been at sea since he was a little boy. (His first voyage had been in a freighter of which his father was the Captain. The Olsens came from Haugesund and all their males were seamen, had always been, right back to the limits of the old ones' memories. It was taken for granted that they always would be, and there was no reason for anyone to doubt it.)

Thanks to the stove, it was warm in the hut. Olsen switched on the main light and began to dress, pulling long seaboot stockings on to his legs before he put on his battle-dress trousers. Then a thick, white submarine sweater and the battledress jacket. It would be cold down on the jetty, at this time of morning, and he could hear the wind bouncing on the hut's round, tin roof. He'd remembered the reason for setting that alarm: a submarine, the *Setter*, was

3

due in from Dundee, on her way to patrol.

That was yet another puzzle; life was full of them! Well, first this business of them taking him out of the 'V' boat just before she was ready to sail for Malta, and moving him up here, to Lerwick. It had come as a shock; he'd settled down well in the new ship, was on the best of terms with his shipmates, and, so far as he'd known up to the moment of being sent for and shown the signal, he'd been performing his duties at least as efficiently as could be expected of a 'new boy'. The 'V' boat's Captain, a Lieutenant not much older than Olsen, had seemed equally surprised at the signal in his hand.

'I've not the slightest idea, Sub. It's – well, that's all there is to it! As you see, it says here they're sending me a replacement for you, but you're to leave without waiting for him. Whatever it's for, it's urgent. You'd better hand over to Number One, and get cracking.' Olsen's disappointment must have shown plainly. The other man, shaking hands with him, repeated awkwardly, 'God knows what it's all about. I'm sorry to be losing you, Olsen. We'll miss you.'

In London, when he reported that evening, they simply gave him another railway warrant, this time to Aberdeen, with instructions to report to S.N.O.'s office for orders. And in Aberdeen they showed him a new signal from Admiral (Submarines), appointing him to the Advanced Submarine Base at Lerwick as Spare Crew Sub-Lieutenant.

To be appointed Spare Crew anywhere was not exactly an indignity, but it was certainly no honour. Compared with an appointment to a new submarine on her way to join the famous Malta flotilla, it was every inch of a long climb-down. It felt like a smack in the face or a kick in the pants, and Lief Olsen, racking his brains throughout the

4

three-day passage (in a trawler) to the Shetlands, could not think of any way in which he might have earned it. He'd been here now, in Lerwick, for a fortnight, and he still didn't know. He liked the place well enough; he got on well with the other officers (there were only five of them, including himself) and with the locals too, or at any rate with the few of them that he'd met. There wasn't much to to do: they, and the sailors of the Spare Crew, were only there to look after submarines in transit between northern patrol areas and the Scottish bases; or, in emergency, to take the place of a man who might fall sick, or be injured, in one of the submarines. Some of them prayed for such an ill wind, which would get them to sea at least for a week or two. Life was easy and comfortable in these heated, well-stocked Nissen huts, but life was also dull. At any rate, it was for the Norwegian.

There were parties, of course. But Olsen was not much of a drinker, and although his English was good he found it tiring to use it day in, day out. It would be so wonderful, he often thought nowadays, to speak your thoughts without having first to translate them; to chat colloquially in your own tongue, instead of forming phrases in someone else's! And it was ruination to any sort of love-life; the strain of talking English to girls, however pretty some of them were, marred the pleasure of their company. He had, in fact, made physical love to only one British girl, and he had done it entirely in Norwegian, and all the time he'd been aware of her constant questioning, 'What? What's that you said? What?' When it was over and his mind had steadied back into its foreign routine, he'd asked her, gruffly, 'What do you mean, *what*? *That's* what!' He had laughed, but she, for some reason, had burst into tears.

He was dressed now, and wondering whether to go

5

straight down to the harbour, or to call in first at the Signals Office to find out how close *Setter* was. If he went straight down, he might hang about on the jetty for an hour before she appeared. If, on the other hand, he went along to the office, he might be late getting down there if she was right on time.

It was a problem. Without having solved it, he put his cap on the back of his head and stepped out into a cold, grey morning. His feet would give him the answer; he would simply follow them.

But there was a much bigger problem, too. It didn't affect him personally, but he disliked questions without answers, and especially now, when there were so many of them about.

The question was this: why was this submarine, *Setter*, going north at this time of year? It was summer, the time of the midnight sun and therefore, for submarines in northern latitudes, the off-season. For a submarine to operate with any sort of safety, there had to be some hours of darkness; she had to surface at night, to charge her batteries, and if there was no darkness she would have to surface, and remain on the surface for several hours of each day (or daylight night, it came to the same thing), in full view of any enemy. And there were plenty of them, around the coasts of Norway.

At this time of year, His Majesty's submarines did not operate in Norwegian waters; yet here was one of them, the *Setter*, on her way north . . .

To Olsen, at any rate, it made no sense. As he passed out through the camp gate, his seaboots clumping on the tarmac and the immediate area washed and tinted in yellow light from the windows of the guard-hut, a sentry saluted him, and Olsen called 'Good morning!' He said it in

Norwegian; it was far too early in the day for linguistic effort.

His boots slithered on the wet cobbles of the street, and he smelt the salt in the wind that gusted noisily at him. It was in his face, which meant it came from the east, roughly: it'd be on *Setter*'s starboard quarter, and he could visualise her, out there in the half-dark, taking it hard as she drove in towards the breakwater. There'd be no shelter for her until she was right inside.

He came down on to the flat, and swung left along the main street, the houses and walls grey, cold-looking, their windows black, as expressionless as the eyes of dead men. (An acre of them, afloat, awash, arched backwards in their lifebelts, salt-washed eyes open, bleakly watching nothing as they rocked to the sea's swell; a long time ago, it seemed, and it shocked him now that he could have half-forgotten it, inside of a year.) Now he turned right and this short street brought him to the quay.

Even inside the harbour the sea heaved, thumping at the granite walls as if it needed more room and resented the confinement. Fine spray stung his eyes as he stared across at the harbour entrance; it was easy to see because the water there was so churned as to be almost white, and to the left of the whiteness he could make out, in the growing light, the silhouette of the end of the breakwater.

'Couldn't sleep, Norsky?'

Olsen spun round, and saw the Gunner, Andy, close beside him, his teeth white in the dark as he grinned with the satisfaction of achieving such surprise. Andy was a small man, and now his stiff oilskins stood round him like a tent so that he looked about as wide as he was tall. He'd been in the Navy for twenty-five years; Olsen knew the round figure because they'd celebrated the anniversary only a week ago.

'Hello, Andy. She due now?

'Any minute, lad. I was watching the entrance there when I see you staggering across the jetty and I thought, blimey, that bugger's still drunk, he's going over the edge . . . You always walk like a crab, Norsky?'

Olsen shrugged. 'So early . . . Andy, you know why she is coming, this time of the year?'

The Gunner coughed hard, painfully, bending forward and banging his oilskinned chest with his fist. When the spasm had passed, he spat carefully to leeward before answering the question that was in his mind, too.

'I only know one thing I didn't know last night, lad; and that's that they've got some sod sick, that's got to be landed. Signal an hour ago, when you was still in dreamland. And I dare say the bloody ambulance has got itself lost, or blown up, or it'd be here long ago.' Andy turned, and yelled into the darkness behind him, 'Parkin!'

'Sir?' A figure detached itself from the corner of the shed, where, no doubt, the four men of the berthing party were sheltering from the wind. Olsen could see the glowing ends of their cigarettes; he hadn't noticed them before. 'Yes, Sir?'

'Send one hand up to 'phone the sickbay. Ask 'em where the bloody ambulance's got to.'

'Aye, sir.' There was a mutter of voices, and movements, then the sound of retreating, clomping seaboots. At about the same moment they heard the engine of the van as it revved and changed into a high gear for the descent of the steep main street. Parkin's voice rose again, recalling the messenger, and a moment later the lights of the ambulance scythed across the jetty, blinding them all as it braked and parked close to the wall where the men were waiting.

Olsen, a faint but obstinate hope stirring in him, asked

8

the Gunner, 'This Signal: they say it is officer, or what?'

'Uh-huh. Just "Request ambulance for one hospital case". What, you hoping?' Olsen grunted, and Andy laughed. 'You've only been here half a dog-watch, chum. You can't be *that* lucky.' He banged his booted feet on the wet paving. 'Bloody cold enough . . . you get it worse in Norway though, I dare say.'

'Very cold sometimes.' It was almost light now; he could see the individual stones in the breakwater on the other side of the basin. 'But not this time of year, I think, so cold . . . There she come, Andy!'

The Gunner'd seen her at the same moment, and he was already yelling at the berthing party to stand by. *Setter* was a cable's length outside the harbour entrance, rounding the last marker-buoy of the swept channel; as she changed course, the sea caught her beam-on, rolling her over until her bridge was almost horizontal, and Olsen, watching, thought, There'll be a mess down there, after that roll. He could visualise the smashed crockery, water sloshing across the deck . . . Sliding feet, and curses . . .

Now that she had her bow lined up on the entrance she was a tiny, swaying silhouette against the sweep of grey sea and dirty dawn sky. The white flashed and spread from her bows and suddenly vanished as her long fore-casing plunged below the broken water; now from here he could see only the gun and the bridge, foam piled round them, and the after-casing, black and naked, slanting upwards: the screws must have been out of water for a moment. Then swiftly she swung the other way, and a moment later the heavy mass of her forepart, that had torn itself free and risen clear of the waves, smashed down like a giant hammer, and she staggered, steadied: and was in the entrance, between the granite walls of mole and breakwater. Men were assembling

9

in her bridge, ready for the order to go down on the casing and prepare for coming alongside. You could say it was light, now, as near as dammit: it was as if the moment of her entering harbour had marked the change from night to day.

. . . .

A bicycle swerved dangerously round the corner and on to the jetty, bringing with it the bulky figure of Commander Grierson, DSO and bar, DSC, Royal Navy. This was Olsen's C.O.; his full title was Senior Submarine Officer, Lerwick. He jammed his bicycle against the wall of the shed, and glanced casually at the parked ambulance; its presence didn't seem to surprise him.

Olsen clicked his heels: as far as it was possible to do so in seaboots: and saluted. A similar sound close by told him that the Gunner was doing the same thing. Grierson flicked his hand up in acknowledgement.

'Morning, Olsen. Morning . . . Who is it that's sick, and what with?' He jerked his head at the ambulance. 'Eh?'

'Don't know yet, sir.' Andrews turned away, and snarled at the Leading Seaman of the berthing party: 'Well, what y' waiting for? Get a line across her bloody bow!' But he'd only shouted because Grierson was there; the sailor had already drawn back his arm, poised himself to send the heaving-line flying out across the gap of water. *Setter* had turned in her own length and was moving in slowly, grouped-down on her motors, at an angle of about thirty degrees to the jetty.

The line streaked out and the weight in its end flipped over the submarine's jumping-wire. One of her casing party grabbed it, and here on the jetty they'd already bent the other end of it to the eye of the wire back-spring. On

Setter's casing they hauled it in smartly until the steel-wire rope reached them: they pushed the eye over the bollard which was there to receive it. Now *Setter* had the spring made fast from her bow to back on the jetty, level with where her stern lay: she'd only to give a touch ahead on one screw, and she'd warp in, alongside. More heaving-lines went out, fore and aft, for the heavy manila ropes which would secure her bow and stern.

Setter slid gently alongside, her saddle-tanks hardly bumping the floating wooden catamarans which were there to keep her off the granite walls of the basin. Andrews told his Leading Seaman, 'Get the plank over, Parkin.' Parkin, who'd already started doing exactly that, allowed himself to glance back, over his shoulder, at the Gunner: then he grinned, tossed the line across, and a moment later they had the narrow plank across the gap from shore to ship; on the submarine's casing a man was busy roping it down.

Grierson advanced to the edge of the jetty and shouted upwards at *Setter*'s bridge. 'MacGregor!'

The submarine's captain was at that moment talking into the voicepipe which connected him with the helmsman down below in the control room. He was saying, quietly, 'Finished with main engines and steering. Fall out Harbour Stations. Open fore hatch only. Nobody's to go ashore and we'll be sailing in four hours' time.' The orders were being repeated back to him out of the brass tube, in the helmsman's voice, as he straightened up and stepped over to the side of the bridge to answer Grierson's hail. Saluting, Lieutenant MacGregor grinned down at the bulky commander on the jetty.

'Morning, Sir. Nice of you to come down at this shocking hour.'

Grierson frowned. 'What's this about a man sick, MacGregor?'

'Sub-Lieutenant Henning, sir. My Torpedo Officer. Looks like his appendix. Luckily it only started late last night.' Grierson saw the other man's eyes shift to look beyond him, behind him on the jetty; he turned, and saw young Braine, the Base Medical Officer, and two Sick Berth Attendants, advancing from the ambulance. Braine had been asleep in the back of it; he'd told the S.B.A.'s to wake him when *Setter* got alongside. Now he told Grierson, 'We'll get him ashore right away, Sir.'

Grierson spoke quietly. 'Yes . . . Braine, you know – '

'I know, sir.' The doctor passed him and went over the plank quickly; he vanished into the fore hatch, followed closely by his two men with their folded stretcher.

Lieutenant MacGregor asked Grierson, loudly. 'Have you got a spare officer for me, Sir?' The commander nodded, and pointed at Olsen, who was standing close to the end of the plank.

'Olsen. Get your gear and report aboard *Setter* inside of thirty minutes . . . ' Olsen started to move, but Grierson added, 'Wait. Come here . . . MacGregor, this is Sub-Lieutenant Olsen, Royal Norwegian Navy.' He told Olsen, 'Lieutenant MacGregor. Royal Naval Reserve.'

Olsen saluted his new C.O. He couldn't keep the happy grin off his face, and MacGregor smiled back. 'Glad to have you, Sub. . . . Look slippy, will you?'

3

OLSEN bent to the rim of the voicepipe and shouted, 'Control Room!' The helmsman's voice answered him, and he yelled, 'Open all L.P. master blows!' The order was repeated back and Olsen straightened, lifted the binoculars to his eyes and resumed the careful, all-round lookout. He was the officer of the watch in *Setter*'s lurching, rocking bridge; they were heading north, on the surface, the diesels churning the screws round at three hundred and eighty revolutions a minute, giving the submarine a speed of advance of about eleven knots. The sea was on the quarter, making it uncomfortable down below in the compartments but comparatively dry up top; plenty of spray, but no green water coming over.

The voicepipe called, 'Bridge! . . . All L.P. master blows open!' and Olsen shouted into the tube, 'Start the blower!' In rough weather, air leaked from the main ballast tanks through the open holes in the bottoms of them; some more air forced into them every few hours brought the submarine up to her normal draft and lessened the discomfort for the watchkeepers. It wasn't only comfort, but the efficiency of the watch; the more spray, the more often a man had to pause in his looking-out to wipe the salt off the end glasses of his binoculars. Olsen let the blower run for five minutes, then had it stopped and the valves shut.

They'd sailed later than expected; topping-up the fresh water tanks and loading fresh stores had occupied most of the forenoon, and MacGregor had decided they'd lunch in harbour and sail after they'd had it. He'd lunched ashore with Commander Grierson, in Grierson's house. Olsen had his in the submarine, with only the First Lieutenant for company; he was a young Englishman named Crawshaw, who'd been at Dartmouth. The other two officers, the navigator and the engineer, went ashore to the Base, both for their own relaxation and to give less work to *Setter*'s wardroom messman.

Crawshaw, the First Lieutenant, was tall, slim and fair; he was younger than the Norwegian, and his air of casual superiority was slightly irritating. He laughed a great deal after saying things that were not, to Olsen, at all funny. When the Norwegian failed to understand a remark, and this happened quite frequently, Crawshaw would repeat it more and more loudly but without any simplification of his vocabulary; and when Olsen still didn't get the sense of the words, Crawshaw'd look cross and mutter, 'Oh, hell, skip it!' Then there'd be a silence until it started all over again. But they were all right talking shop, because Olsen knew the words.

The voicepipe called again. Olsen bent to it: 'Bridge.' The helmsman asked him, 'Permission to relieve lookouts, Sir?'

That meant it was just on six, and the watch changing. They'd left harbour at about two, and the First Lieutenant had taken the watch until four-thirty (the officers changed over half an hour after the rest of the watch) when Olsen had relieved him for the two hours of the First Dog. Now, about half an hour to go, and from now until they got back from this patrol, or whatever it was, it'd be two hours on and four hours off, all round the clock.

During the afternoon the captain, MacGregor, had been working at the chart table, and in the tiny wardroom

Olsen spent the time getting to know the navigator, an R.N.V.R. Sub-Lieutenant called Soames, and the engineer, a Keyham lieutenant with the odd name of Massingbird and a jutting red beard. Soames told him that the beard looked red now, all right, but that long before the end of a patrol it was a dirty brown colour from the oil which it gathered while its owner was peering into pieces of machinery.

'Bridge!' He answered again, stooping: 'Bridge.' A new voice reported 'Helmsman relieved, Sir. Course oh-oh-five, three-eight-oh revolutions.'

'Very good.' Olsen pulled a wad of damp periscope-paper out of the pocket of his waterproof Ursula suit (so called because this sort of protective clothing had been designed by a man who, at that time, was commanding a submarine named *Ursula*) and cleaned the glasses of his binoculars for about the fiftieth time in a hundred minutes. He glanced round at the lookouts: they were the reliefs, who'd just come up, but muffled in their protective clothing they looked exactly like the two who'd gone below: both of them had their glasses at their eyes, slowly turning as they swept the broken, heaving line of the horizon. The safety of the submarine and the lives of all the men in her depended entirely, at this moment, on those eyes, on theirs and his; on their seeing any enemy or sign of him before that enemy saw *Setter*. It meant continuous lookout, utter concentration, from each of them for the whole two hours of the watch. Braced between the sides of the bridge and the periscope standards, shiny-wet already from the flying spray, they seemed rooted to the ship itself as it pitched, rolled and staggered; only their heads and shoulders and arms moved as they pivoted slowly, searching the sea and sky.

A dozen feet above the top of the after periscope standard, a solitary gull kept perfect station, floating, gliding, never moving its great, spread wings. Now and then it tilted to a changing gust of wind, and its head moved jerkily, suspiciously, as if it were keeping a close watch on the submarine and on her every movement. The gull had been there when he'd taken over the watch, and it hadn't changed its station by an inch.

The diesels rumbled steadily into the spreading wake, driving *Setter* northwards, towards the circle of the midnight sun.

.   .   .   .

'How's the weather, Sub?' MacGregor asked the question from his bunk as Olsen stopped in the gangway opposite the wardroom space, shedding his wet Ursula suit and making puddles on the deck as the water ran off it.

'Better, Sir, I think. Wind dropping a little and I think the sea going down too.'

'Thank God for that.' The Captain rolled over on to his back and went on reading his thriller. The engineer was turned in, too; only Crawshaw sat at the wardroom table, entering figures from sheets of paper into some sort of ledger. Probably battery readings. Olsen hung the two parts of the waterproof suit on hooks behind the heavy bulkhead door (which was kept latched back and shut only in emergencies, Collision Stations and Depth Charging) and slid himself on to a bench at the table.

The wardroom was no more than a square alcove off the gangway that ran the length of the submarine; it could be shut off from it, when anyone wanted to, by a curtain which hung from a rail on the deckhead. It held five bunks: the Captain's, by itself on the for'ard bulkhead, two against the curving starboard side of the pressure-hull, two more on the after bulkhead. Of the latter pair, the lower one belonged to the engineer, and the upper was his own.

Olsen hadn't asked anyone, yet, what *Setter* was going north for, in the off-season. He'd hoped that someone might have volunteered the information. Since they hadn't, he decided to ask.

'Captain, Sir.'

'Uh?' MacGregor turned his head and looked at him.

'This is a bad time for northern waters. Can I ask what we are going for?'

MacGregor grinned. He shoved the novel down the side of his bunk, swung his legs out and slid down to sit on the bench facing Olsen. It was something of a gymnastic feat, the way he did it.

'You can ask, Olsen old chum, but I'm buggered if I can tell you.'

'So.' Olsen nodded. That was that!

'But I'll tell you one thing you *don't* know, and as everyone else knows it I dare say it's time you did.' Olsen watched his face, waiting, and the Captain went on. 'You aren't here by accident, and Henning, the chap we landed in Lerwick, hasn't got a damn thing wrong with him. It's a put-up job, you might say; and pretty bloody stupid, too, the way they complicated it.'

Olsen couldn't think of any suitable comment. He waited; the Captain fished a tin of cigarettes out of a drawer behind him, under the bunk, and offered them round. Crawshaw shook his head, but Olsen took one and produced matches.

MacGregor blew a cloud of smoke at the overhead lamp, on which someone had pasted labels off gin and whisky bottles.

'We were on patrol, you see, near Wilhelmshaven, and they recalled us suddenly to Dundee. We'd only been on the billet a day. When we got in, I was told we had to do some special job up this way; we had thirty-six hours in Dundee and shoved off again for Lerwick. If some stupid bastard in the Admiralty had realised we were going back into Dundee you could have been sent to join us there. But they sent you up to Lerwick, a week ahead of us, instead . . .'

The Captain drew hard on his cigarette. 'If they've half a chance to tie a thing up in knots, that's what they do.' Suddenly he looked round and shouted, 'Ellis! Where's our supper?'

The wardroom messman, a skinny seaman in overalls, stuck his head and shoulders round the bulkhead doorway. 'Won't be long now, Sir. Soup'll be up in a couple o' minutes.'

'Soup?' Crawshaw glanced up from his figures. 'What sort of soup, Ellis?'

The messman shrugged. 'I dunno what *sort* it is, Sir. But it smells —ing 'orrible.' He withdrew, and MacGregor grinned at the First Lieutenant, who'd only raised his eyebrows and gone back to work.

'Well, Olsen, I don't know what this job is, but apparently we have to have a bloke that can talk Norwegian. For some *other* reason they didn't want us to take an extra man: so the answer was to swap an officer. All that bull, pretending Henning was sick, was laid on by some cloak-and-dagger expert who reckoned that if we swapped you two over openly, in Lerwick, some fifth columnist or whatnot might hear of it and get an idea we were going to – well, do whatever we bloody well *are* going to do. Obviously we're going to get within at any rate hailing distance of someone who talks your language, so one might reasonably imagine

18

that we'll be going close inshore somewhere.'

Olsen hadn't taken in every word, but he had the gist of it. MacGregor pointed at the chart table. 'Give me the chart that's under the top one, will you? . . . That's it. Now . . .' He spread it out on the table. 'Look. We've got to hang around – *here*. It's about three hundred miles from Lerwick, so we'll be there tomorrow night. Not that there'll be any night, in the true sense of the word.'

Olsen checked quickly. The place the Captain had marked with a small pencilled cross was roughly latitude 65 north and longitude 5 east. His eye travelled to the familiar shape of the Norwegian coast, and he thought, about a hundred and fifty miles north west of Trondheim – which the Germans are using as a base for some of their U-boats . . .

MacGregor was saying, 'We've got to wait there and try not to get spotted until we get a signal giving us further orders.' Olsen looked up from the chart thoughtfully, and the Captain added, 'And that's all I can tell you, because it's all I bloody well know.' He stubbed out his cigarette, and muttered, 'How the hell we avoid getting spotted when there won't be any dark hours, they didn't try to explain.'

'Supper's about on, Sir.' Ellis was back; he waited while Crawshaw collected his paperwork and Olsen removed the ashtray (which had the name of a Gibraltar hotel around its edges), then flipped a more-or-less white cloth across the table. When he'd smoothed it down, it was less white where his hands had touched it. MacGregor frowned.

'Ellis. Before you do anything else, go and wash your hands.'

The messman seemed surprised. He said, 'Conserving fresh water, Sir. First Lieutenant's orders.'

'Go and wash, Ellis.'

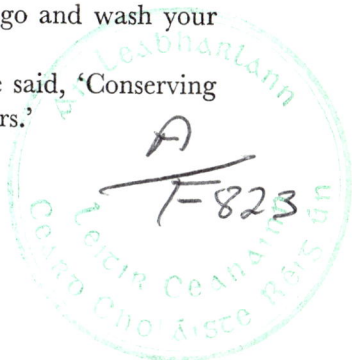

'Aye aye, Sir.'

In a minute he was back, flipping down spoons, knives and forks as if they were cards he was dealing. Olsen looked at him, and Ellis said, 'Nothin' up me sleeves, Sir. It's the quickness of the 'ands deceives the eye.'

Massingbird, the engineer, climbed wearily out of his bunk, and sat beside Olsen, yawning and scratching his beard. He peered through half-closed eyes at the table, and murmured, 'I can't understand why that man gives us forks for sardines, when he knows damn well we only spread 'em on bread.' He stared morosely at the First Lieutenant, holding him responsible, and Crawshaw asked him,

'How d'you know it's sardines?'

'Can't you smell the bloody things?'

'Soup, Sir.' Ellis plonked down two cups in saucers, and went back to the galley for more. Crawshaw said, 'It's the soup you're smelling, Chief. It's made of bad fish.'

The Captain sniffed at his, and tasted it. 'I think you're right, Number One. Bad fish.' But he went on sipping it, and Ellis brought in the other two cups. He asked the Captain,

'All right, Sir?'

'No. What is it?'

'I reckon it's several things, Sir. Kind of a mixture, like, as the Chef thought of. It smells –'

'—ing awful. You were quite right.' MacGregor had cut him short. 'Ask Chef what it is.'

'Aye aye, Sir.' The messman went away, and they heard muttering in the galley, next door. Only the Captain and Olsen were drinking the soup; the other two had pushed their cups into the middle of the table, and Chief had his eyes shut.

Ellis came back, and coughed. 'Chef says it's *Potage Maison*, Sir. 'E says the recipe's secret, like...' The messman stared solemnly at Crawshaw. 'It's frightenin', ain't it, Sir?'

After supper (the rest of it was mutton and roast potatoes: they'd got the fresh meat in Lerwick), the Captain struggled into an Ursula suit and, muttering, 'Get some fresh air before I turn in,' left them. Olsen heard the helmsman call up to Soames, on watch, 'Bridge! Captain coming up, Sir!' Anyone except the Captain needed the officer of the watch's permission to go up; and usually, if the submarine was in an area where the enemy might be encountered, the O.O.W. would restrict such visitors to one at a time. If you had to dive in a hurry, you didn't want a whole mass of people queuing to get down through the hatch. Two lookouts and one officer made quite enough of a crowd if you were going to submerge in twenty seconds flat; and twenty seconds could feel like as many minutes if there was an aircraft dropping on you from the clouds. (The aircraft didn't even have to belong to the enemy: the friendly sort were just as dangerous. To most pilots, any submarine was a target to be bombed.)

Crawshaw muttered, 'Anyone mad about fresh air, he can keep my watch for me.' He was working at his record-book again, but he'd be on watch in forty minutes. When he came off, at ten-thirty, it'd be Olsen's turn again.

Olsen considered the idea of trying to get a couple of hours' sleep. But he wasn't tired yet, and he knew he'd only lie there and think about this extraordinary trip, and wonder what they needed him for. It was no good theorising: when the orders came, the answers wouldn't fit any of the guesses. It'd be either disappointing, or just plain terrifying. And as to that, nobody with any imagination at all could feel exactly nonchalant about the plans as they were already known; to hang around, for considerable periods on the surface, in daylight, within long-range spitting distance of a busy U-boat base – well, that was enough to start with.

Olsen pulled some files and looseleaf notes out of the drawer where they were kept by Henning, the man whose place he'd taken. He browsed slowly through them, stopping at points of interest to study the things he felt he should know about: the detailed orders for such evolutions as Gun Action or the despatch of a Boarding Party – which would be his job. He checked through the Torpedo Log, which contained a record of the maintenance routines carried out regularly on each of the submarine's torpedoes. She carried thirteen: six in the bow tubes, ready for firing, six reloads in their racks in the Fore Ends (which was where most of the crew lived), and one in the solitary stern tube – the sting in *Setter*'s tail. In the same book were the names and personal details of the torpedomen, starting with the T.I., a Chief Petty Officer named Rawlinson. (T.I. stood, oddly enough, for Torpedo Gunner's Mate. A T.G.M. used to be called a Torpedo Instructor, and now the name had been changed but the old letters stuck, to baffle foreigners like Olsen.)

Olsen had talked things over with Rawlinson, before they'd sailed from Lerwick; he was a tall, rather silent man, with the best part of a lifetime of Naval service behind him. What the talk had boiled down to was that the department was secure in Rawlinson's seasoned and very capable hands and that so far as he, the T.I., was concerned, it wouldn't make much difference if the Torpedo Officer was a Chinaman with two heads. Rawlinson hadn't said that, of course, or anything like it. It was simply there, and both of them knew it.

'First Lieutenant, Sir.' A messenger had come from the Control Room. 'Ten minutes, Sir.' Crawshaw glanced up at him, then at the clock on the bulkhead. He sighed.

'All right, Baker. Thank you.' As the messenger turned away, he bumped into the Captain, who'd just come down from the bridge.

'Oh, sorry, Sir! I didn't –'

'Think nothing of it.' MacGregor grinned at the seaman. 'How's that redhead of yours, Baker?'

'She's all right, Sir, thank you.' Baker left, chuckling to himself. MacGregor dragged his arms out of the Ursula jacket. 'She certainly *is* "all right".' He waved his hands in the air, indicating the shape of an hourglass, and told Olsen, 'She's really *something* . . . You're on watch in a couple of hours, Sub. Better get your head down, hadn't you?'

Olsen nodded. He'd been thinking of it. The Captain added, 'Dare say we'll be ducking up and down rather a lot, after tomorrow. I'd get all the zizz you can, if I were you.'

.   .   .   .

Olsen pulled off his rubber-soled, canvas shoes; he stood up on the bench he'd been sitting on, and taking great care not to disturb the engineer who was asleep in the lower berth, he prepared his bunk for occupation. This wasn't a long job. The bedding, neatly stacked, consisted of two blankets and a single pillow; he spread one of the blankets out, double, with the fold against the bulkhead and the open edges facing him along the side of the bunk, and pushed the pillow in between the two thicknesses at the head end. The other blanket went on top, doubled. Olsen folded back the three upper thicknesses, and climbed in. He took his shoes with him, and stowed them under the pillow, where he'd find them easily instead of having to grope about on the floor; turning-out in an emergency was a hellish enough business without having to grope around on the deckboards, banging your head on the legs of the table and against the heads of three other people doing the same thing. In small spaces, life was easier for the man who organised his movements in advance . . .

The Captain was already turned-in, motionless, perhaps even asleep. Olsen stretched out to the lamp that hung over the table, and switched it off. Then he drew the curtains along the side of his bunk, lay back, and closed his eyes.

It was a strange feeling, to be shut out of your own country, to know it was full of Germans, and to be going, now, so close to its shores. Not that he had people there – not close ones – to think about. Most of his friends had been at sea when the balloon went up, and, like him, they'd stayed out. As for his family – well, there weren't any, really. His father had died a year before the war began, and his mother'd been dead for five years before that. He'd no brothers, only a sister, and she was in Australia. Two aunts, and an uncle who was a retired whalerman, had been alive three years ago; but it was two years since he'd written to them, and there'd been no answer to any of those letters.

No girl friends, either. Except – well, the one he sometimes thought of at moments like this, times when he wanted to think about his own people, stake a claim in memory if nothing else to a past which was fragmentary and which largely eluded him. He'd been abroad so much, even before the war. And tankers spend little time in their home ports.

He didn't even know her name. She had a face, though

24

it floated in his memory (or was it in his imagination, the result of his *trying* to see it?) somehow *bright*, always, as if when he thought of her there was a spotlight that caught the high, smooth forehead, the small, well-shaped nose and soft, wide mouth. Her hair, he knew, was blonde and fine – contrasting with his own, which was dark and very thick – and her eyes were . . .

Half asleep, he battled for the colour of her eyes. They'd be blue, with that hair. But they weren't blue. Grey? Brown? He was straining to see and to know as he sank into sleep, but the girl's face was only a splash of light, an aura; to try and bring it into focus was like trying to close your hand on smoke.

Vaguely, at a distance, he heard Soames kicking off his seaboots, turning in, and he thought, reluctantly, It doesn't matter. She'll be someone else's girl, by now . . . Although, while he couldn't get her face clear, couldn't see her eyes at all, he could hear her voice so clearly that she might have been talking with her lips against his ear!

He fell asleep smiling, liking the things she said.

4

GREY cloud ribbed the sky like the underside of a tattered awning; *Setter* rode the long, flat swell easily, the sea hissing back in foam swirling along her saddle-tanks, spreading white from her gently heaving bow as it lanced the smooth, grey-green surface.

It was mid-morning, and Olsen had the watch, keeping a look-out that was tense, urgent in its concentration, more so even than usual, because a light mist restricted visibility. It was like straining your eyes to see through a wet handkerchief: Olsen was very much aware that if he saw anything, it wouldn't be far away. And these were enemy waters.

The two seamen lookouts were up on the small platforms which projected from the tops of the periscope standards. In normal conditions, the extra ten or twelve feet in eye-level gave a longer range of horizon; now, in fog, it put the men's eyes above the worst of it. The Seamanship Manual was quite clear on the point that in such conditions lookouts should be stationed high up or low down, to see either over or under the fog. So there they were; but there was one serious disadvantage in it. If you had to dive the boat in a hurry – the operation which films and newspapers invariably called Crash Diving – it would take just that two or three seconds longer for the lookouts to get down and through the hatch.

But you couldn't have your cake and eat it.

.   .   .   .

The watch changed at noon, and Olsen, after the usual exchange of reports and requests through the voicepipe, continued his binocular search of the shrouded horizon. He heard the lookouts changing over behind him, and the new men climbing up on to the standards; the ones going off watch reported to the back of his head, 'Lookout relieved, Sir,' and he muttered, 'Very good' without taking the glasses from his eyes or pausing even for a second in the pure concentration of visual effort.

One of the things they taught you, in the training course, was that when you were on watch you should constantly think of the many possible emergencies: the sighting of an enemy ship, a periscope or the track of a torpedo: think of each thing in turn and decide in your own mind what action you'd take, what orders you'd give, immediately and almost automatically, if it *did*. You would not, for instance, take the same action if you saw an enemy on your beam as you would if he appeared right ahead ...

The idea was that these mental rehearsals would leave you ready for split-second reaction to any sort of emergency. But the drawback was that when you're constantly *imagining* an enemy, it isn't difficult, especially in the dark or in fog, to believe in the figment your own mind has created. Most submarines have been dived more than once for aircraft that have turned out later to be seagulls.

It was for this reason that when Olsen saw the U-boat he did not, for a moment or two, believe his eyes. Catching his breath and feeling a sudden pounding in his blood-pressure, he made himself move the binoculars on, just past it, to get that darkish grey image in the edge of the circle of glass: then sweep back the other way, to see if –

It hadn't faded. The U-boat's bridge was tall, narrow; her casing, almost bows-on to *Setter*, low and indistinct. But unmistakably the fog-smothered silhouette of a submarine, fine on the starboard bow, and *Setter* perhaps ten or fifteen degrees on the enemy's port bow ...

'*Dive, dive, dive!*' As he shouted he dropped the glasses on their leather strap around his neck, twisted round to face the lookouts and dropped one hand on to the bar that would close the valve on the voicepipe. The two men flung themselves down, grunting with the effort of sudden fast movement, acrobatics almost: their faces were distorted in surprise and with the alarm of knowing there must be some menace close, but not knowing *what* danger or *how* close. A dozen feet straight drop from the periscope standards down on to the platform of the bridge: then heavy, hard breathing, cluttered in seaboots and protective clothing, one on top of the other, cursing, into the oval brass rim of the upper hatch.

He hadn't needed to repeat the emergency diving order into the voicepipe: the helmsman heard it when he shouted to the lookouts, and the submarine was already going down, sinking, the deck of the bridge angling under his spread feet. The big vents had clanged open in the tops of the saddle-tanks, and the spray plumed up, whistling and roaring, like half-a-dozen whales spouting all together, only much more noisily: the diesels had stopped and it was the electric motors now that were forcing *Setter* downwards as she nuzzled into the sea. Spray from the vents was falling on Olsen's head and he could hear the rush of rising water, bubbling, as he shut the valve on the voicepipe and jumped into the hatch on top of the second lookout, dragged the heavy lid down above his own head and engaged the clips, leaning his weight forward to push them home hard. While he did it, one of the lookouts shouted up, 'Captain says, What's up, Sir?'

Olsen yelled down, 'U-boat on the surface, green one-oh, two miles about, coming towards.' He heard the Captain snap 'One hundred feet.' The boat was steeply angled and as Olsen stepped off the bottom ladder into the Control Room the needles in the depth-gauges were swinging past forty feet, which put them well underneath any torpedoes which might have been coming their way.

The Captain murmured, 'Group down,' and Sellers, the yellow-haired man who worked the telegraphs to the motor room, jerked the handle over. 'Grouped down, Sir, both motors full ahead.' The Captain told him, 'Half ahead.' He glanced at the depth-gauges: sixty feet, sixty-five ... He told the Outside E.R.A., 'Blow Q.'

'Blow Q, Sir.' Featherstone opened the valve to let high-pressure air into "Q", the quick-diving tank, which, flooded, was pulling *Setter* down fast. He kept his hand on the valve until the light flashed, then shut it and reported, 'Q blown, Sir.'

'Hutchins.' MacGregor was talking to the man in the corner who wore headphones and worked the Asdic set. Hutchins was a tall, thin seaman with a long, blue jaw: squatting on the stool behind the set, his knees stuck up like masts. He saw the Captain speaking to him, and pushed the 'phones off his ears.

'Sir?'

'Hear anything?'

Hutchins shook his head apologetically. 'Not yet, Sir.'

'Listen all round for H.E.'

'Aye aye, Sir.' He clamped the headset back over his ears and bent over the dial of his instrument, slowly turning the knob.

The two 'planesmen – hydroplane operators – were easing the dive as *Setter* approached the ordered depth. The Cox'n, Chief Petty Officer Bird, was working the after 'planes, and the Second Cox'n, a leading seaman named Hallet, chewed mournfully on some unknown substance as he manipulated the other wheel. There was a depth-gauge in front of each of them, and a spirit-level between them. Bird had taken the angle off by using his 'planes to bring the stern down, and now Hallet adjusted carefully to settle the needle in his gauge at exactly one hundred feet. As if the achievement depressed him, he reported, gloomily, ' 'Undred feet.'

'Slow, Number One, when you can.'

Crawshaw glanced at the bubble in the level, at the steady gauges and the indicators which showed the 'planes were more or less horizontal. He told Sellers, 'Slow ahead together.' Sellers whirled the handles of the telegraphs.

'Slow ahead together, Sir.'

MacGregor had gone over to the Asdic corner, and he was bending beside the set, wearing the spare set of headphones. Presently he took them off, and shook his head. 'Olsen – you *sure* you saw a U-boat?'

'Sure.' He added, 'Sir.'

The Captain shrugged. 'Thirty feet. Half ahead together.' He muttered half to himself, half to Crawshaw, 'We'll have a butcher's.'

As the submarine rose towards periscope depth, Mac-Gregor waited beside the big brass barrel of the for'ard periscope. He glanced at Featherstone, and flicked his fingers upwards; the E.R.A. raised a steel lever and the periscope rose, hissing, from its well. As the lower end of it came to chest level, the Captain grabbed the folded handles and jerked them down; Featherstone lowered his lever and the periscope thumped to a stop. MacGregor put his eyes to the lenses and waited.

The needles swung slowly round the gauges, and as *Setter* rose past fifty feet, forty-five, forty, the men in the Control Room who were watching the Captain's eyes could see the greenish light reflected in them and brightening as the upper lens approached the surface; at thirty-three feet, the light changed suddenly to white.

Crawshaw reported, 'Thirty feet, Sir.' He was busy at the switches over his head, the electric telegraph which flashed his orders to men on the pump and at the valves of the internal ballast tanks: as the submarine rose, she got lighter, and you had to pump water out of those tanks to keep her at neutral buoyancy. Archimedes thought it out, more than two thousand years ago.

The Captain spun quickly, hanging on the handles of the periscope; a rapid all-round search of sea and sky. Then he started again slowly, carefully, hunched and concentrating, his left arm hooked right over the handle, like an ape in a tree. When he'd been all the way round (every man in the Control Room who didn't have an instrument to watch had his eyes fixed on him) he stepped back, his face expressionless. He pushed up the handles and gestured to Featherstone, who sent the brass tube hissing down into its well.

'Number One. We'll stay down for lunch, then surface again until evening. Hands to Watch Diving.'

'Aye aye, Sir.' Crawshaw asked Bird, 'Which watch, Cox'n?'

'Blue, Sir.' Crawshaw lifted the microphone of the broadcasting system off its hook, and switched it on. His voice echoed through the compartments. 'Blue Watch, Watch Diving. Blue Watch, Watch Diving.'

MacGregor put a hand on Olsen's shoulder. 'Don't worry, Sub. Better dive for a Flying Dutchman than stay up and get fished.'

Olsen didn't argue. He *knew* what he'd seen, but there was no point in repeating what nobody would believe; he nodded to the Captain, and moved up beside Crawshaw to take over the watch again. He was thinking. Perhaps the German saw us and dived at the same moment, and our Asdics just didn't hear his motors. There had to be some explanation; he thought, whatever it is, that Asdic set isn't much bloody use.

It was a disturbing thought.

.   .   .   .

Although Olsen would have been off watch at twelve

thirty, his having dived the boat had prevented Soames getting any food in time to take over. So the Norwegian kept the dived watch while the others lunched, and had to postpone his own until they surfaced again.

Lunch was corned beef, and peas out of a tin, followed by a square of hard pastry with red jam on it. He was alone at the wardroom table; Chief was in the engine room, Soames on watch, Crawshaw asleep with his curtains drawn, and the Captain up topsides, getting some fresh air and adding his eyes and binoculars to the afternoon watch. 'Getting fresh air' was his excuse for being there; in fact, he was worried. Not entirely convinced that Olsen's U-boat had been a figment of the imagination, in spite of what he'd said (what else could he have done – put salt on its tail?) he was very much aware that German submarines based on Trondheim, which was now a major base for their Atlantic patrols, would be more than likely to be passing through these waters on their way out or coming home. MacGregor would have liked to have stayed submerged; but he wanted to be sure of getting to the waiting position that evening, and he felt, too, that as they'd have to spend several hours of each 'night' on the surface in broad daylight, and even closer to Trondheim than they were now, it didn't make much odds if they took that same risk now.

'More, Sir?' Olsen looked up at Ellis, who was offering him another slice of the jam-coated pastry. 'Plenty if you want it.'

'Thank you. Yes.'

The messman's finger pushed it off the dish and on to the Norwegian's plate. Instead of going back to the galley, he rested one hand on the end of the Captain's bunk and began to make conversation.

'You think that really was a —ing U-boat, Mr Olsen? What you saw?'

'Sure. Big one.' Olsen raised his hands and spread them as if he was indicating the size of a fish. The messman whistled.

'Well, — me. What d'you think 'appened to the —er, Sir?'

Olsen grinned at him. '—ed off, I think.'

Ellis nodded, as if the explanation satisfied him. 'Ah. I 'spect you're right. That's what I'd 'a' done, if I was 'im. I wouldn't 'ang around, like.' Olsen went on eating his pastry; out of the corner of his eye he saw Ellis shamble for'ard, and a moment later he heard him repeating the conversation, word for word, to the chef. When he came back, he brought with him a cup of warm liquid which tasted like a mixture of tea and cocoa, but which in *Setter*, so Olsen had learned, was known as coffee.

Olsen slept until teatime, then read through some back numbers of *Good Morning* until it was time for him to go back on watch. *Good Morning* was a sort of newspaper, the copies undated but numbered, which the *Daily Mirror* produced free of charge and supplied to submarine flotillas. The papers were handed out each morning by the Cox'n, day by day in numerical order. They couldn't carry news, of course, in the way a proper newspaper does, but they had pin-ups and strip cartoons and photographs of submariners on leave drinking beer in Fleet Street pubs with the editor and staff of *Good Morning*. Olsen found the words simple and the text easy to follow; when he came across a word he didn't know, he looked it up in his pocket dictionary.

. . . .

Setter stayed on the surface all that night. She passed through her waiting position at about two thirty in the morning, but MacGregor had decided to carry on northwards to the top edge of the allotted area so that the next day's dived patrol could be on a southerly course and bring her back to the centre, the cross on the chart. He wanted to be there around midnight each night, because it was at that hour they could expect the signal to come, when it did, and then they'd be right on the spot – or within a few miles of it – where the Admiral (Submarines) in his head-quarters at Northolt would expect them to be.

By diving at five in the morning, *Setter* would have a run back of twenty-five miles, which would be just about the right distance: twelve hours at an average speed, dived, of about two knots. The aim was to spend a maximum of time under the water, and during that time to go as slowly as possible so as to conserve the power in the batteries. That way they'd need comparatively few hours on the surface, re-charging.

The necessity to surface to charge the batteries was the great limiting factor in submarine operations. It meant, in fact, that a submarine was not a true *submarine* at all, but only a craft which could submerge for limited periods. When the scientists or the engineers one day reversed this situation, produced a true underwater ship which could surface when it needed to but not because it had to, then, for the first time, that would be a submarine. And present conceptions of naval warfare would be knocked into a cocked hat.

Olsen came off watch half an hour after midnight on this second morning out of Lerwick. By the time he'd entered his weather report in the log, drunk a cup of the Cox'n's cocoa (which was called *kye*: another absurdity which a foreigner could only accept because if he asked for an explanation he'd almost certainly find there wasn't one) and got himself under the blankets in his bunk, it was one o'clock. So he had three hours' sleep until they shook him again, soon after four. At four thirty he was on the bridge, taking over from Crawshaw, and twenty minutes later the voicepipe barked, 'Bridge!'

He bent to it. 'Bridge.'

'Captain coming up, Sir.'

MacGregor clambered out of the hatch and stood beside him. 'All right, Sub?'

'All right, Sir.' Both of them hunched over the front of the bridge, scanning a grey horizon and a gently moving sea that shone slickly as if it had had a dull, half-hearted polish; like shoes left outside the door in a second-class hotel.

'Go on down, Olsen. I'll dive her.'

'Aye aye, Sir.' He let himself down into the hatch, into the hard, noisy rush of air that the diesels were sucking in. In the Control Room, Leading Seaman Hallet asked him, 'Diving now, Sir?'

'Soon.' He stood near the ladder, waiting, and the lookouts came down, their boots clomping awkwardly on the steel rungs. The Captain's voice broke out of the voicepipe close to the helmsman's ear.

'Stop together. Out both engine clutches . . . Open main vents.'

Five o'clock: the patrol proper had begun.

5

I t was seven in the morning and they were starting breakfast. Half an hour ago Soames had taken over the Control Room watch from Olsen, and the silence from that direction was broken only by his voice as he occasionally gave a quiet order, and by the hiss and thump of the periscope as it was raised and lowered every few minutes for a search of the sea and sky. The soft hum from the motors was scarcely audible; *Setter* was going slow ahead on one screw only, creeping south at periscope depth.

It was just a matter of waiting, of passing a day.

'Come on, Chief. Wakey-wakey!'

The figure in the lower bunk rolled over and peered through half-open eyes at the three of them sitting round the wardroom table. He groaned, and his hands came up out of the blankets to cover his face while he yawned.

'What for?' Crawshaw had pulled back the curtain which shielded the engineer's bunk, and the influx of light seemed to be causing him discomfort. Crawshaw told him, 'Breakfast, Chief. Cornflakes and lovely tinned milk. Good for growing boys.'

'Oh, God!' Chief moaned again as he dragged himself up on to one elbow. He looked awful.

Olsen asked, 'He is ill?'

The First Lieutenant shook his head. 'He's always like this, first thing. Suicidal. I bet his wife hopes the war'll go on for ever.'

'Get out of the bloody light, will you?' Chief was

struggling out of his bunk and on to the bench, and Crawshaw slid along it to make room for him.

MacGregor told the engineer, 'I spent a few days in an American accommodation ship, once. Had to sleep in a sort of dormitory. When the chaps turned out in the morning they used to do exercises, and shout "Hurray for me, hurray for I, another chance with life to vie!" I'll write it down for you, Chief, so you can start the day off right.'

'I don't want to start any bloody day in any way at all . . . Ellis!'

The messman stuck his head round the corner. 'Coming, Sir. Coming.'

MacGregor turned to Olsen. 'Whereabouts in Norway d'you come from, Sub?'

'From Haugesund. You've been there?'

'No. Nice place?'

'Small harbour. Lot of fishing boats, coasters. It's a long time now I am not there.'

Ellis brought in the main course, which was tinned sausages and tomatoes. Chief turned his head away from the sight of them. Crawshaw told him, 'I'll have yours, Chief, if you don't want them. We haven't *all* had twelve hours' solid sleep.'

Chief ignored him, and told the Captain, 'Those American friends of yours'd bloody well mutiny if they had to eat Soya Links six times a week. They get chicken and sweetcorn and all sorts of things, turkey and eggs and bacon, in their submarines. Even the Germans get special food, on patrol.'

'Where the hell d'you get that information?'

The engineer was helping himself to bread and butter and marmalade. 'Ellis – coffee, please. Even if it *is* made

37

with tea leaves, I want some now, not next week ... How do I know it? I read it, in the papers. Their submarine crews live off the fat of the land. Treated like heroes. Fêted in Berlin when they get back. I read about it ... How you can stand the smell of those things, Number One, let alone *eat* them, I can't think.'

Crawshaw told Olsen, 'He eats them, at lunchtime. It's just the mornings ... Have you got any family, in Haugesund?'

Olsen shook his head as he spooned sugar into coffee. 'No. My father and my mother died before the war started, and the others – there's a long time, you see, I am away from Norway –'

'No girl friends?'

Olsen considered the question seriously. It linked in with things he thought about. He'd have liked to say yes, and for that to be the answer, but –

MacGregor, who'd noticed the hesitation and the doubt, and who in any case felt chary of asking questions about a man's family and friends in an occupied country, broke in so that Olsen wouldn't have to answer.

'How about Lerwick? You like it there?'

'Not so much. I do not like to be ashore, so much. I was at Blyth ashore, you know, and now I like to be at sea again.'

(They heard Able Seaman Baker telling the chef, 'If there's any —ing Links left, cock, we'll have 'em for'ard. Right?' Then Ellis's voice, growling that he hadn't had *his* —ers yet, so those —ers up for'ard could keep their bloody 'ands off 'em, or he'd —ing well do the lot of 'em, so 'elp 'im.)

'The language in this ship,' observed Crawshaw, 'leaves a great deal to be desired.' He asked Olsen, 'Do they use as much foul language in Norwegian ships, or is it just a British habit?'

'Oh, yes.' Olsen nodded, seriously. 'The words, some of them, not so different, either. I think it –'

'Captain, Sir!' Soames' voice was hardly raised, but the note of slight urgency carried it clearly to the wardroom. MacGregor slopped his coffee as he dropped the cup into its saucer and shot quietly but with considerable speed and agility out of the cramped space, into the gangway, and aft into the Control Room.

'Yes?'

Soames had just sent the periscope down. He told the Captain, 'Aircraft, Sir, seaplane. On the port quarter, quite a long way off, moving left to right.' MacGregor must have gestured for the periscope, because they heard the hiss of it rising as Soames added, 'Angle of sight about ten degrees, Sir. It's not close.'

Sound of the handles clicking down, then a pause, and MacGregor's voice ' 'M . . . Down periscope. Sixty feet.'

'Sixty feet, Sir.'

'Stay there ten minutes, Sub. Then call me and we'll have another *shufti*.'

.   .   .   .

By the time Olsen came off watch at half past twelve they'd seen two other aircraft, and each time they went deep for a spell to make sure they weren't spotted. The frequency of these air patrols annoyed and worried MacGregor. For one thing, it was abnormal to see so many planes so far offshore, and that gave him an unpleasant feeling that the enemy might be on the alert – for what? And the other thing was that while it wasn't difficult to see them a long way off, through the high-powered periscope, and to get down out of all danger in plenty of time, it'd be much less fun later on when they'd have to be on the surface. It would mean frequent alarms, broken sleep for the men off watch – or even none at all – and having to dive periodically would interrupt the charging of the batteries so that they'd have to spend even longer, over all, on the surface. A vicious circle – and, of course, so far as the enemy was concerned, half the object of the operation . . .

MacGregor told himself that the patrols probably had nothing at all to do with *Setter*'s presence in the area; that this was probably just an unlucky patch and they mightn't, after this, see another plane for days and nights on end. He was uncomfortably aware, though, that this was wishful thinking.

Olsen turned in after lunch. The atmosphere in the dived submarine – the silence, the warmth, and the steadiness of the ship as she patrolled thirty feet under the surface – was very conducive to sleep. Particularly when nobody ever had longer than four hours off watch, and cutting off the bits at each end of those periods (getting turned-in, and then getting awake again before the next watch) it meant, in fact, that the longest period of actual sleep, all through a patrol which could last three weeks or more, was three hours. No one had any trouble from insomnia.

Ellis produced tea and biscuits at four in the afternoon, and at twenty past the hour Olsen shuffled into the Control Room to relieve the First Lieutenant. He learnt that the course was the same – due south – and that *Setter* was going slow ahead on the port motor only. Depth ordered, thirty-two feet; the Captain's orders, to show as little periscope as possible.

The trim seemed perfect; the hydroplanes were horizontal, except for an occasional tilt of a few degrees on the for'ard pair; the bubble was half a degree aft of the centre-line, and both depth-gauges showed that the submarine was exactly at the ordered depth. Crawshaw told him, 'She seemed a bit heavy aft, an hour ago, but I reckon now she's right to the nearest pint.'

Olsen took a quick look all round through the for'ard periscope. Nothing in sight: there was no more than a gentle lop on the sea. Just enough to give tiny patches of white everywhere, the ideal conditions for submarine patrol. Calm enough to keep depth accurately without any effort, and that broken surface to camouflage the trace of the periscope when it showed.

He nodded to the First Lieutenant. 'O.K., then.' Crawshaw went to have his tea; it was exactly four thirty.

Remembering those instructions from MacGregor that he was to be careful with the periscope, Olsen put it up and down more frequently than usual but for shorter periods. From thirty-two feet there couldn't be much of it showing, in any case; and if it was never up for long, well, supposing that he'd missed seeing an aircraft and that now it was close enough to see the periscope, by the time the pilot took a second look it'd be gone. The odds were thousands to one against *Setter* being spotted, in these conditions.

It occurred to Olsen that MacGregor must be worried; and the thought surprised him. That burly R.N.R. Lieutenant with his easy manner and calm, brown eyes, struck the Norwegian as a man who'd have to be very hard-pressed indeed before he'd lose any sleep . . . But, of course; he'd said to Olsen, when he'd been telling him about this trip, that their orders were to hang around and at all costs to avoid being seen. He was making sure of that – no more.

41

Olsen had been watching the trim; now he turned and moved towards the periscope. He raised his hands slightly, curling the fingertips upwards, and the E.R.A. of the watch eased up on the lever of the hydraulic gear which operated the periscope.

First, the very quick all-round look in low power; without the magnification, you could fairly whirl round for that preliminary check before you switched (by moving the motorcycle grip on the left handle) to high power for the much more careful but still – remembering those orders – fairly rapid search.

Olsen was halfway round in low power when they heard him gasp. The E.R.A. and the messenger of the watch, and the Asdic operator (all of whom, at their stations, faced into the centre of the Control Room) were already watching him, lazily, disinterestedly; now they jerked upright, their eyes suddenly wide open, and the other men in the compartment, too, twisted round to look at him. They saw his left hand jerk over to flick in the magnification, and immediately after that his two hands snapped the handles up and the E.R.A. had the periscope hissing down before the Norwegian's mouth had opened.

'Diving Stations: port twenty, steer oh-three-oh; half ahead together: stand by all tubes –'

Orders being repeated and men running and confusion (it *looked* like confusion, but it wasn't, it was urgency and the need for speed) and MacGregor there with Olsen telling him, 'U-boat, Sir. Bearing oh-nine-five and we're thirty on his port bow. Twenty of port wheel on, course ordered oh-three-oh. We're grouped down, half ahead together, thirty-two feet.'

The periscope was shooting up into the Captain's hands and the man beside the helmsman reported, 'All tubes

42

blown up, Sir . . . All tubes ready, Sir.' He wasn't on his stool yet but he had the headset with the 'phones against his ears and at the other end of the line was Rawlinson, the T.I., in the tube space right for'ard. At this end it was the signalman, Wyllie.

MacGregor muttered, 'Bloody good, Olsen.' He was bent double at the periscope because the rush of men aft from the for'ard compartments had left *Setter* light in the bow, and she was above her ordered depth; Crawshaw was battling to adjust the trim but meanwhile MacGregor didn't need the periscope right up and he didn't want to show even six inches more than he had to. He snapped, 'Start the attack. Bearing – *that!* We're – yes, thirty on his port bow. Range – *that.*' He read it off and sent the periscope down. Olsen had the picture set, now, on the Fruit Machine, a mechanical box full of wheels and dials: you fed in the data and it gave you the figures you needed for the shot. MacGregor said, 'Steer oh-three-five. Set enemy speed fifteen knots, Olsen. What's my D.A.?'

The Norwegian read it off his machine and MacGregor told the helmsman, 'Steer oh-three-two . . . Up periscope.' He pushed the hair back off his forehead and muttered, '*It's a gift. A sitting bloody duck!*' He wasn't talking to anyone except himself. The periscope rose into his hands and he started again, 'Bearing – *that!* I'm – fifty on his bow. Range – *that!* Down periscope, group up.'

Soames, working the plot on the chart table, now had two sets of ranges and bearings on the target. He set his calipers between the points and then against the scale in the corner of his plotting diagram. 'Enemy speed, seventeen!'

MacGregor told Olsen, 'Set seventeen. D.A.?' Olsen gave him the new angle of aim-off, and MacGregor said to Wyllie, 'Tell the T.I. I'll be firing six fish. Stand by.'

Wyllie passed the message into his telephone, MacGregor was looking down at the stopwatch in his hand; he'd started it at the moment he'd said 'Start the attack,' and Soames had set another watch going simultaneously. Eleven minutes ago . . .

'Up periscope.' The Captain studied the enemy for a moment, checking that she hadn't altered course or speed, that she was where he'd expected her to be after this exact interval. He took his eyes away from the lenses and turned the periscope to set it at the Director Angle which Olsen had obtained from his machine. MacGregor bent to the periscope again, and muttered, 'Down a bit, down . .' Featherstone dropped it gently, slowly, about six inches.

'Stand by . . .'

Crawshaw was tensely watching the depth and trim. If he let the boat go below her depth now, he'd dip the top of the periscope under water and ruin the attack possibly just at the moment of firing. If he let her come up, suddenly, the enemy might spot the periscope, and that, too, would wreck everything.

'Fire one!' Wyllie yelled it almost in one voice with the Captain. The submarine jolted, trembled, as the first torpedo thudded out of its tube.

'Fire two!' Pressure rose sharply as the compressed air which was used to drive the fish out of its tube vented back into the submarine. 'Fire three! . . . Fire four!' Hutchins, the Asdic man, reported, 'Torpedoes running, Sir.'

'Fire five!' (MacGregor thought, Running – thank God. Just let 'em run *straight*!) The U-boat's stern had passed his aiming line by a full length and a half again, and he yelled 'Fire six!' He clicked up the handles and Featherstone pushed the lever down hard.

All through *Setter*, men were swallowing to clear their

ears from the suddenly increased pressure. MacGregor stood absolutely still, his eyes on the watch in his cupped hand. He knew the distance-off-track and hence, at forty knots, the running time of the salvo that was on its way. Hutchins said quietly, 'All torpedoes still running on course, Sir.'

'H'm.' A dozen pairs of eyes were on the Captain as he slipped the stopwatch into his pocket; shouldn't there've been a hit, by now – if there was going to be one?

'Up periscope.' MacGregor grabbed the handles as if he were drowning and needed them to save his life. Stooped, with his eyes at the lenses, his mouth was drawn back tightly at the corners: he was thinking, *one hit, that's all it needs* . . .

It came. It jarred *Setter*, rocked her so that the 'planesmen had to fight to keep her down. Fragments of paint and cork chips rained from the deckhead.

MacGregor's breath came in with a sharp hiss. He whispered, '*Ah, my God!*' They watched him, their faces alight with excitement. 'Number One. Quick – take a look. She's going!' Crawshaw jumped to the periscope but he was too late. Disappointed, he stepped back, shaking his head. The Captain told him, 'Right amidships, under the bridge. Blew her in two and the two halves were up-ended and going down separately and bloody fast.'

Now there was a silence in the Control Room. In a few minutes, they'd be delighting in the kill. A U-boat dead was part of a convoy saved. But now, with the crash still ringing in their ears, they were aware more than anything else that the ship they'd blown apart and sent to the bottom was a submarine, not much different from this one they lived in themselves. There couldn't possible be a survivor and it was unlikely that there'd be even a single complete

45

body in the twisted shell that was on its way, at that moment, to the sea bed.

MacGregor lifted the microphone off its hook. He switched it on, and tapped it to make sure that it was working; the taps boomed out of the loudspeakers.

'D'you here, there. We've just sunk a U-boat. We scored one hit amidships and she sank in two parts . . . Fall out Diving Stations. Watch Diving.' His tone had been flat, quite unemotional, and to look at his face as he turned away nobody would have known that he'd just won himself an automatic D.S.O.

6

Setter surfaced that evening at eight fifteen: Crawshaw had the watch, then, from eight thirty, in greyish light from the continuous but invisible sun which, if it would have shown itself through the haze, would have been low on the northern horizon.

MacGregor's orders to officers of the watch on the surface during the six hours' scheduled battery charging were that they were to keep the ship under almost continual helm, steering an erratic series of zigzags, circles or figures of eight, never allowing a straight course for more than two minutes. In this way no enemy submarine could do to them what they'd done to the U-boat, earlier in the afternoon – except by a fluke, or by using a homing torpedo, and although it was reported that the enemy had such things and had used them occasionally against our Atlantic convoys, it was also reported they didn't often work.

All the same, there was an atmosphere of tension down

below. To be on the surface in daylight in enemy waters gave an uncomfortably naked sensation to anyone who thought about it; and the feeling of unreality was increased by the frequency of helm orders down the voice-pipe and the list, now and then, as *Setter* swung sharply on to a new course.

The on-edge feeling added to the satisfaction of having sunk the U-boat, and the result was a submarine full of men who laughed and talked more than usual, in louder tones than they normally used; jokes came easily, and up for'ard a group of men off watch were singing ribald songs.

They'd had supper soon after surfacing, and now with coffee still on the table MacGregor had brought out some poker dice and they were playing Liars, with match-sticks for stakes. Chief, who was in exceptionally high spirits, was by nature a bad liar, and he lost a life at almost every round. Quite often he'd lost three, and was out, before anyone had lost one at all. It didn't seem to depress him, except that he told them more than once, quite cheerfully, that it was a childish, stupid game. Olsen, who had learnt it when he was at Blyth and played it there and in Lerwick, did well; he was aided by his limited knowledge of the English language. He stuck to logic and observation and remained unbaffled by misleading remarks which he often failed to understand.

That flatness which had descended upon them after the destruction of the U-boat, had gone altogether. They'd talked about it, and what was more in their minds than anything else now was a mental picture of Atlantic convoys, tankers going up like torches in the wild, cold night, men dying, families bereaved, food and war material going to the bottom. That U-boat had been heading out from Trondheim, bound for the Atlantic to contribute her

torpedoes to the deaths and losses and destruction. Well –
men would be alive, in two weeks' time, ships would be
afloat, women ashore would have no cause to weep; food,
weapons and munitions would be off-loaded in British
ports; and they could thank, for all of that, the salvo
Setter fired this afternoon at ten to five.

.   .   .   .

The tubes had been reloaded. After the attack, *Setter* was
taken down to a hundred feet while it was done. First the
Fore Ends, the compartment where the reloads were
stowed and where the crew lived, was cleared out; everything – hammocks, the long table, mess gear, boxes of
stores – was shifted into the gangway and into the other
messes. Then Olsen crawled for'ard over the heaps of
gear into the compartment, and watched the T.I. and his
torpedo men perform the evolution of reloading the six
tubes. It was a heavy, complicated business, moving the
torpedoes out of their racks, jockeying them into position
and then hauling them by block-and-tackle into the tubes;
a job that would have been difficult under any circumstances but which in that cramped space required meticu-
lous care, a great deal of intelligence and massive combined
strength. If a wire was led on the wrong side of a stanchion,
or rove the wrong way round through a sheave, and someone failed to notice the mistake at once – well, you'd carry
on for half an hour and have a couple of fish out of their
racks and you'd find, suddenly, that that was as far as
anything would move; the next half-hour would be spent
not only cursing but also undoing everything that had been
done so that it could all be started again from scratch, and
this time the right way about. And if a man put foot or
hand in the wrong place at the wrong time, he could get

three tons of torpedo down on it without any trouble at all except the loss of the limb.

Nothing did go wrong. They were a well drilled team, this bunch, thoroughly practised, and Rawlinson saw every move a full minute before it was made. When they'd finished, and Olsen went to report to the Captain that it was done, MacGregor glanced at the clock and raised his eyebrows.

'Good going, Sub.'

The Norwegian had had very little to do with it, but since he was the Torpedo Officer the Captain's comment made him feel on top of the world. And he'd learnt a great deal, too, because this was the first time he'd seen it done, under patrol conditions.

He lay in his bunk now, thinking about it. He'd turned in to sleep, when they'd finished the dice game, thinking he'd get an hour and a half, or nearly, before his next watch. But his mind was churning around, seeing things happen all over again, and now half an hour later he was still wide awake. There'd –

'Engineer Officer, Sir!' It was a messenger, trying to wake Chief: nothing had kept *him* awake. 'Lieutenant Massingbird, Sir. Signal for deciphering. Engineer –'

'Uh? What's that? What signal?'

'Cipher, Sir. Addressed to us, P.O. Tel says.'

One of the Chief's few jobs (apart from keeping the engines running, which could be a sleepless one for days on end when the diesels were being temperamental) was to cipher and decipher coded signals. He always needed another officer to help him – one to read the coded groups and one to look them up in the books – but it was his responsibility, and here in the messenger's hand were several pages of signal-pad covered with groups of letters

49

which had come over the air in a rapid stream of dots and dashes and of which Chief must now, immediately, make sense.

'All right.'

Olsen peered over the edge of his bunk, parting the curtains, and saw a long, scrawny arm stuck out of the lower berth, grabbing the sheets of pink paper. Chief himself followed the arm, and switched on the overhead lamp.

Soames climbed out of his bunk against the ship's side. 'I'll give you a hand, Chief.' At the same moment, the Captain arrived; he'd been on the bridge, with Crawshaw, and the Petty Officer Telegraphist had told him through the voicepipe of the signal's arrival.

'Where's this signal, Chief? You got it deciphered, yet?'

Chief ignored the dig. Soames had taken the keys out of the Captain's drawer and gone into the Control Room to get the cipher books out of the safe. MacGregor looked up and saw Olsen watching him over the edge of his bunk; he hadn't moved, his English wasn't good enough for this sort of thing. MacGregor said, 'Well, Olsen; perhaps we'll get the answers to all those questions of yours, out of this lot.'

Soames came back, with the heavy books in their lead-weighted covers; the idea was that they'd sink easily, if there was some danger of them falling into enemy hands. And of course, if a ship was sunk, they wouldn't float to the surface.

(With that sort of contingency in mind, there was also an enormous demolition, or self-destruction, charge at the after end of the Control Room. The circumstances under which this might be set off, and by whom, to blow the submarine apart, were left to the imagination of the submariners.)

Chief began to read out the signal, one code group at a time. As Soames gave him the interpretation from the book, he wrote it down, a word or a phrase at a time, on another signal pad. MacGregor sat facing them across the ward-room table; he was smoking a cigarette, his chin resting on his left fist.

The first words were, YOU ARE TO RENDEZ-VOUS. MacGregor grunted, and slid out around the edge of the table. He switched the light on over the chart table, and turned to look at Soames.

'Come on. Where?'

'Not where, Sir. *When . . .*' He told Chief, 'AT 1000 HOURS GMT – .' Chief wrote that down, and read out more letters. Soames added, '21 JUNE.'

The Captain murmured, 'That's the day after to-morrow.' He made his own note of the date and time. Soames went on,

'IN POSITION –' and the next bits of translation gave a position in latitude and longtitude. MacGregor bent over the chart, and Olsen climbed down from his bunk to go and have a look. Soames announced in a tone of excitement,

'WITH – FISHING BOAT –'

Chief, scribbling, muttered, 'Well, — me!' Mac-Gregor told him, 'No thanks, Chief. Not even in Scapa.'

'FLYING –'

'*What?*'

'Flying. One word. *Flying*. Got it?'

MacGregor moved sideways, and showed Olsen the rendezvous position which he'd marked on the chart. It was thirty miles offshore, roughly level with their present position.

Soames announced, 'WHITE FLAG.' The next

group was a full-stop, then came the word E MBA R K. The Captain came back, and sat down. He looked depressed.

'Hell. Passenger. He'll have to have your bunk, Chief, there's nothing else for it.'

Chief muttered, 'Like hell he will –'

'BISHOP –'

'Bishop?'

'Bishop, Sir. Look.' MacGregor checked the group, and nodded.

'Well, I'll be –'

'Spelling, now . . . D –' . . . It came out slowly, and it added up to the word DALEN. They checked it carefully, and MacGregor asked Olsen, 'Is that a Norwegian named, Dalen?'

'Oh, yes. Means in English, valley. Many Dalens, in Norway. This bishop –'

Soames interrupted. Chief's pencil was poised, and the navigator told him, 'AND – WIFE –'

They looked at each other, and Chief said, slowly, 'A bishop and his wife – *here*?'

'Seems like it. Come on.'

The next word word was AND, and MacGregor's eyebrows shot up. Hadn't they got enough?

'DAUGHTER –'

'Oh, *no*!' MacGregor stared at Soames, as if it was his fault. 'Are you sure?'

'Positive. But you can check it, Sir.'

'No. Go on . . . oh, my God!'

'AND –' MacGregor began to laugh. Olsen, looking at him, caught the infection, and joined in. It spread to the others, and the messenger came through from the Control Room to see what was the matter. He went back and told the helmsman, 'They're all gibbering, in there.'

Soames could hardly get out the next word: it was ATTENDANT. MacGregor was almost choking. He gasped, 'In the singular? Hasn't he got the choir with him?'

Soames looked up from the cipher book. He closed his eyes, and controlled himself with a great effort of will. He said, quietly, 'PRIEST.'

Olsen broke into the ensuing silence to finish what he'd been about to tell them, a minute ago. 'Bishop Dalen, I know of him, He is with the Norwegian Resistance. He was put in prison twice already by the Germans. Very good man, I think.'

MacGregor nodded, 'I hope he's a very *slim* man, too.'

The rest of the signal was more straightforward; the whole message read:

You are to rendezvous at 1000 hours GMT 21 June in position latitude 65° north longitude 11° east with fishing vessel flying white flag. Embark Bishop Dalen and wife and daughter and attendant priest. Thereafter proceed Lerwick utmost despatch. Report success of operation when clear of Norwegian coast. Time-of-Origin, 2129/19.

MacGregor muttered, half to himself, 'Well, now we know . . .' He looked up at the electric clock. 'Olsen, you're on watch at ten thirty; d'you mind going up now? I want to talk to Number One about all this.'

'Sir.' Olsen squeezed out past the engineer.

.   .   .   .

Olsen told the helmsman, 'Ask permission, please, for me to relieve officer of the watch.' The man looked surprised, and glanced at the clock before he yelled the request up the voice-pipe. There was a pause, no doubt a repetition of the surprise; then the answer came, 'Yes.' Olsen grabbed the sides of the ladder and struggled up hard against the rush of air.

(A couple of hours ago, when they'd surfaced, the air-rush had been in the opposite direction. With the high pressure in the submarine after firing six torpedoes, Mac-Gregor'd had a man hang on to his legs as he opened the top hatch, to hold him down. Otherwise he'd have stood a good chance of being blown out like a cork the minute he took the clips off the hatch. It had happened, in other submarines, and to careless captains.)

'You're early, aren't you?' Crawshaw hadn't taken the glasses from his eyes; the two lookouts were just as intent on their job, and the ship was steadying after a violent turn to starboard.

'Yes. Captain wishes to speak with you about Bishop Dalen.'

'Bishop – *how much?*'

'It is in the signal . . . Better the Captain explain, I think.'

A minute later, Crawshaw dropped into the hatch while *Setter* performed a neat circle and, at Olsen's order into the voice-pipe, shot off tangentially to turn the figure into a Q with a long tail. Down below, the automatic plot under the chart table was keeping track of each movement; it would show, at any time the information was wanted, *Setter*'s relative distance and bearing from the starting position. An allowance would be made for the current (from the tidal chart of the area) and the result of all that would be what is known as a D.R. (Dead Reckoning) position. Later, Soames would try his sextant on the few stars which showed in this light – well, only the North Star, but with it the planets Venus, Mercury and Mars, if they were in the mood. You couldn't hope to see much else, and even if the sun were visible for long enough to shoot it, the angle would be so low that you'd need to take a dozen sights and use the mean of them all. Through this haze, even that would be unreliable.

Olsen thought, as we go closer inshore, soundings will be a help. The charts show the changes of depth, the contours of the sea bed, and with the echo-sounder picking up the shape of it we'll get a check on where we are. He bent to the voicepipe and ordered, 'Port fifteen.'

'Port fifteen, Sir.'

'Steer one-one-oh.'

So – Bishop Dalen! Mrs Bishop Dalen, and – the name that came to him was Ingrid. Not that it was she – the Bishop's daughter. It was just that in the back of his mind there was a link, a feeling that the girl – she, Ingrid – the girl he often thought about, girl out of a dream – that she'd had a father who was a –

Clergyman? Could – now – be a bishop? But he'd known of this Dalen, ever since the war started every Norwegian had known of him, and it had rung no bell before. Could it be that the name meant little because it was a distant sound, echo of a man walled-in and far away and, more than that, a figurehead, a hero, so that he remained a name and not a man at all, more a legend and a father-figure and – to say it truly – doomed?

'Starboard ten.'

'Starboard ten, Sir . . . Ten of starboard wheel on, Sir.'

More likely, this. That the thinking, those dreams willed on in daylight, the needing to think and doing it because of that, wanting a fixed mark at which to aim the thoughts like the stake you flung the horseshoes at – you

55

and this recollection of a girl whose name now suddenly was Ingrid: but had you ever heard it? Did you know her, years ago? Or see her, passing, observe and pass by, and since then linger, looking back, but only afterwards? Then the face was a dream, and the name a myth . . .

If you tried hard, you could remember names of girls in Cape Town, Buenos Aires, Suez, Bombay, Colombo, Sydney and a dozen other ports. Girls very much like each other: you could have swapped them round, jumbled them up and dropped them like pegs or puppets into each other's worlds, and no one would have noticed, or, if they had, much cared.

Only this one: she, presented suddenly, tonight, with the very ordinary name of Ingrid –

'Midships.'

'Midships, Sir . . . Wheel's amidships.'

'Steer north.'

'Steer north, Sir.'

– which, no doubt, had never been hers and which she'd have hated to acquire, even in a daydream from a man she'd probably never seen and almost certainly never noticed: she – so, call her Ingrid – could not transfer, was incapable of being confused with any of those others whose names and faces, figures, were quite definite, remembered, names and dates and places and differently accented words pathetic in their miserable similarity.

'Port twenty.'

'Port twenty, Sir . . . Twenty of port wheel on, Sir. Permission to relieve lookout?'

.   .   .   .

Those extra forty-five minutes made it seem like half a day he'd been on watch, by the time Soames came club-bering out of the hatch. He told Olsen, 'There'll be a mutiny in this hooker, by midday.'

'So?' Olsen had the glasses at his eyes; they'd been there, with hardly a break, for more than two and a half hours. He searched slowly down the port side as *Setter* steadied on a new course. 'For what?'

'Captain and Number One spent an hour nattering. More. After you came up. Then Number One wrote out a lot of bloody stupid orders and I had to type 'em out. I only finished half an hour ago – the typewriter doesn't work and every couple of lines I have to take the spools off and rewind the ribbon, or what's left of it.'

'You could put a new ribbon?'

'Oh, yes. But it tears down the middle. I don't know why. ... We've got to stop swearing.'

'Swearing? Stop –'

'Words like — . There's a page about it. They're putting swear-boxes all over the boat and there's a price on every word. Captain's going to make a speech, in the morning, and after that it'll cost poor old Ellis a bob every time he opens his mouth. They don't want to offend this bishop chap, you see ... And the lads've got to dress properly, too.'

'*Uniform?*'

'Hell, no. But they aren't allowed to walk through the boat without trousers, and buttons undone, and that sort of thing. Women, you know. I can see the point – as things are usually, they'd get some pretty nasty shocks.'

'Where shall they sleep?'

'That's all worked out. Captain keeps *his* bunk, and Chief'll have a camp bed in the Control Room, poor old sod. You and me and Crawshaw'll share your bunks – yours and Chief's – and work "hot bunks". One of us on watch all the time, you know, so when you go off you take whichever of the two's empty. The bishop and his priest chap'll have Number One's and mine.'

'But the women?' Olsen bent to the voicepipe. 'Starboard ten!'

'Petty Officer's Mess. All to themselves. They're going to rig up a canvas screen for it, inside the curtain, and the P.O.'s'll overflow into the E.R.A.'s Mess and one or two of 'em in the gangway. Hot bunks for them, too.'

'This seems all right, don't you think?'

'Ah. But it's the language thing that's going to annoy 'em. Can you imagine the Cox'n, or the Stoker P.O., never saying — ?'

Olsen chuckled. 'The bishop would not mind such words, here. He is half a soldier, in a way . . .' *Setter* had turned through ninety degrees or more. Olsen yelled down, 'Midships!' He asked Soames, 'You taking over, now?'

Down below at twenty-five minutes to one, Olsen entered his weather figures in the rough log, and accepted a cup of cocoa from the P.O. of the watch. It was blistering hot, and by the time he'd drunk it and got himself into his bunk it was nearly one o'clock. He'd be shaken at four fifteen for his next watch, so that meant three hours' sleep. As he lay back and closed his eyes, he told himself that the first night they were back in harbour he'd be in bed by eight in the evening, and make sure of remaining unconscious for a solid twelve hours. But even as he made the resolution, he knew he'd never keep it. No one ever did. That first night in was always a late one, and there was always a hangover on the morning after. It was the second night in that did you good.

The messenger roused him punctually, and at half past four he took over the watch from Crawshaw. There'd been no excitements or alarms, and the orders were still the same:

to keep a sharp lookout and an erratic course. But the Captain had left orders to wake him at twenty to five, so presumably they'd be diving soon.

Olsen noticed three or four gulls following the ship. There'd been none yesterday. He was pleased to see them, partly because like most sailors he regarded them as friendly creatures, and even more because he felt that these must be Norwegian birds, the first he'd seen for several years. He waited until Crawshaw had gone down into the hatch, then shouted loudly to the nearest of them,

'Good day, my friend!'

The bird screamed, and banked away, and one of the lookouts jerked his head round.

'Sir?'

'Nothing . . . Nothing!'

There was a gentle swell on the sea, but the surface was smooth, unbroken. A bad surface for periscopes . . .

'Bridge! Captain coming up, Sir.'

'Very good . . . Port twenty.'

'Port twenty, Sir. Twenty o' port wheel on, Sir.'

MacGregor climbed out of the hatch and came to lean against the front of the bridge beside the Norwegian. 'Morning, Sub.'

'Morning, Sir.' He bent, and shouted, 'Midships!'

MacGregor told him, 'Come round to three-two-oh, Sub.'

'Aye, aye, Sir. Control Room – port ten!'

'Port ten, Sir. Ten of –'

'Steer three-two-oh.'

MacGregor told Olsen, 'I'm going to dive on the klaxon. Shake 'em up a bit. You go on down, now.'

Olsen dropped into the hatch and lowered himself towards the Control Room. First, there was that hatch

59

which opened into the bridge; it was called the conning tower hatch, and once inside it you were in the conning tower itself, a vertical tube with a ladder up its side and another hatch, now open, at its lower end. Through this lower hatch you came on to another ladder which slanted down to the deckboards of the Control Room.

The red-painted push-button of the klaxon was just below the top hatch. The first lookout was stepping off the bottom ladder when MacGregor jammed his thumb on the button, twice: the klaxon bellowed, an ear-splitting, shocking noise that brought men out of their bunks and hammocks so fast that there might have been flames in the seats of their pants. Olsen, who'd been peeling off his outer clothing while he waited for that horrible din to shatter the warm silence in the wardroom, grinned to himself as he saw Chief's usually inert body come flying out of its hole in the blankets. The engineer's hair was standing on end, his beard jutted like a shaggy bowsprit, and his eyes were wide with alarm. He flung himself into the gangway and collided heavily with Leading Seaman Hawkins, who was proceeding aft at the double but with his eyes only partially open. Both men swore violently as they ploughed on like interlocked forwards in a rugger game.

When *Setter* was steady and level at periscope depth, MacGregor reached for the microphone of the Tannoy broadcasting system, and addressed the ship's company.

'D'you hear, there? Now, listen carefully. We've had our orders, by signal last night : . .'

He told them about the fishing boat they had to meet, and the passengers who'd be coming aboard.

'This means we've got all of today just to hang around and stay out of sight. We'll surface tonight at eight, and we'll spend eight hours going flat out for the rendezvous position. Then we'll dive at four, or five, depending on how we get along, and five or six hours dived'll bring us there at ten o'clock. That's tomorrow morning.'

The Captain paused, and cleared his throat.

'I personally intend to shave tonight. And I want to see clean chins on every one of you by nine in the morning. Everyone, that is, except the engineer officer.' MacGregor glanced aft in the direction of the engine room, and Chief, who was standing in the entrance, grinned at him.

'Second thing: *language* . . . ' *Setter*'s ship's company listened with occasional comments as their captain lectured them on personal cleanliness, foul language, and the wearing of trousers. When he'd finished, he said,

'That's all. Watch Diving – carry on.'

As the men changed round and those off watch went back to their messes to catch another hour's sleep before breakfast, there was very little conversation: it was as if they didn't trust themselves to speak.

7

I T was the loft of a fisherman's cottage and he'd used it to store sails in, sails and rope and all sorts of gear, nets and lanterns and lobster pots, canvas bundles of Lord knew what. The loft ran all across the top of the cottage, so it was a biggish room, long and narrow, the length of two rooms and a passage and the width of one. The trapdoor was right in the centre of it, and, at the moment, shut.

At each end of the loft was a very small window, a fixed pane of glass in a heavy frame which wasn't made to open. These windows admitted very little light, partly because they were so small and also because the other cottages had their end walls close up to them, a few feet away; on the ground there was only a narrow path dividing each cottage from the other. And the panes were dirty, too; salt-caked on the outside and lined on the inside with a tangle of cobwebs.

Bishop Dalen sat between his wife and daughter on a heap of old canvas. It had been comfortable enough at first, and they'd even slept for an hour or two, tired out after several days on the move and the last half-day jolting along in the back of an ancient lorry that stank of fish. But they'd been here since before midnight and the bed of sails felt very much less resilient than it had at first.

The bishop wrinked his nose at the smell of fish which still clung to his clothes, and for about the hundredth time he'd said it in the last week he murmured, 'I'm sorry to be going, now, leaving all – all –' he waved his hand, indicating not the loft around them but all of Norway to the north and south and east. 'I wish it wasn't necessary.' He spoke quietly, so as not to disturb his daughter; she was still fast asleep with her head resting on her crossed forearms, her body curled in a circle like a whiting's; long, blonde hair spread all across her face, hiding all of it except the tip of her nose.

Mrs Dalen sighed, and took her husband's hand in both of hers. 'I know. But I, Eric – I am thanking God for it.' She looked down at their daughter, and added, 'I shan't sleep until we're away, afloat in this submarine.'

The bishop smiled. 'You told me you would be frightened of it, a fortnight ago. To go under water.' And he thought, but didn't say, she was as soundly asleep as Kari, an hour ago!

'I would spend the rest of my life under water, holding

my breath or whatever we have to do in that thing, rather than stay and have them – the Gestapo – *you*, in their filthy hands –'

She was crying, at the thought of it. He put his arm around her shoulders and pulled her closer, whispering in her ear that she needn't be afraid, they *were* going, in a few hours they'd be on the last lap; it was over, the fear and the hiding, the years of nights she'd lain awake, listening and waiting for the crashing on the door, the shouts . . .

Twice, that had happened. Both times, he'd come back to her. But if there should be a third time, the Dalens knew there would be no return. Before, it had been the Military Government. Now, the bishop's affairs had been handed over to the Gestapo. They'd ordered his arrest, and prisoners of the Gestapo did not return to their families. When a case was placed in the hands of those gentlemen, it meant that a decision had been reached, probably in Berlin. A decision which would deprive the Resistance of their spiritual leader.

The bishop found a handkerchief in his pocket, and placed it in his wife's right hand. It was not very clean, the handkerchief, and he was glad of the poor light which disguised the greyness of the linen. She was always so particular about those things, and he'd got into trouble more than once by absent-mindedly hanging on to the same handkerchief for two or three days.

'I wish we could –'

'Sh!' His hand tightened on her shoulder, and he whispered, 'Someone's coming, I think!'

Footsteps, loud on the bare, wooden stairs. No voice. The steps halted, shuffled away, came back; they heard movement just under the trap-door and then the scrape of the ladder being dragged across the landing. The bishop leant down, and gently shook his daughter's arm.

'What? Father! Is –'

'Be quiet, Kari. Somebody is coming. Don't make a sound!'

The end of the ladder thudded into place below the trap-door, and they heard the scrape of feet as someone climbed it. The square of boards rose an inch, then swung up, and a man's head and shoulders appeared in the gap.

'It's me – Kjellegard.'

'Delighted you've come at last. Do we go now? Where's Bjorn?'

'Bishop – I'm sorry. Sorry to have to tell you . . . They've got him.'

'*No!*' Mrs Dalen pressed the handkerchief against her mouth, and the bishop felt her body trembling in the circle of his arm.

'Wait – hush!' He patted her as if he was calming a nervous horse. He said to Kjellegard, 'Now, please explain. *Who* has got him, and how, and where?'

The man came up through the trap and dropped the cover back. He squatted on his heels, facing the bishop. 'All right. But we've only got a minute . . . The Gestapo took him. If I'd been there it wouldn't have happened. He had some worry about the fuel and he persuaded one of my people to take him down to the boat. They were waiting there and got them both. The place is swarming with police, they've got wind of something. So – I'm sorry, but we have to change our plans.'

'We're – not going?'

'Certainly you are going, Mrs Dalen. But not tonight, and not quite as we had planned. There is an alternative. Now, Anna is coming here for you, at any moment. Go

64

with her, do exactly as she tells you, and I'll be meeting you again tomorrow. With luck, you'll only be delayed a day.'

The bishop nodded. 'That's all right, of course . . . But, Bjorn –'

'No, Sir. Just the three of you. There's nothing we can do about the other. Nothing. If there was, we'd do it. Believe me, you must go now, without him. There's no alternative.' He swivelled round, and pulled up the trap-door. 'I'll lead. Then you, Madam, and your daughter. Bishop, if you'd let this thing down over your head as you come down, it'll save me coming up again.'

When the bishop joined his wife and daughter on the landing at the head of the stairs, between the two upper rooms, Kjellegard jerked the ladder away and stowed it inside the door on the left. As he rejoined them, the street door opened; a woman stepped in and shut the door quickly behind her. She stood waiting, looking up as Kjellegard led them down the stairs.

'Well done, Anna. Everything all right?'

'Yes.' Anna had a shawl round her head and a rug-like coat over her shoulders for protection against the early morning cold. She curtsied to the bishop, and smiled at the two women.

The bishop told her, 'It is good of you to do this for us, Anna.' Kjellegard put a hand on his arm, drawing him aside.

'Eh?'

'That man of yours, Sir. Could you – you'd say he's –'

'He is a priest. He is also a very strong man. I mean, in his mind. He has risked his life many times for many people – including myself.'

'Then –?'

65

'They won't get anything from him. That's what you mean?'

Kjellegard looked away. He said, 'You'd better start now, Sir.'

Mrs Dalen asked him, 'Can't you come with us, instead of meeting us tomorrow? If they're here in the village, they might – you might get –'

Kjellegard shook his head, politely, but with a trace of impatience. 'I know how to stay out of trouble. And I've work to do: to start with, a message to London . . . Please go, now.'

The bishop nodded to Anna. 'We're ready. You'll lead?' He patted Kjellegard on the shoulder. 'Au revoir, then.'

Kjellegard closed the door behind them. He was thinking, that transmitter's forty miles away. I need an aeroplane, or at least a car, and all I've got is Anna's bicycle . . .

He was tempted to use the telephone, but that was out of the question and it made him angry that he'd even thought of it; with this flap on, the village filling up with black uniforms and jackboots, they'd be sure to have all the lines tapped.

He hadn't mentioned to the Dalens that a patrol boat had arrived among the fishing craft along the jetty. It was a fast looking launch, bristling with machine guns.

8

Setter was at periscope depth and Olsen had the watch still. The course was north west; they'd hold it until mid-day and then come round to due east so that when they

66

surfaced that evening they'd be on the eastern edge of their waiting area, with a few miles start for the run-in to the coast.

At the after end of the Control Room, Wyllie, the signalman, squatted on the deck sewing one edge of a sheet of canvas on to a length of hemp rope. This was to be the screen for the Ladies' Boudoir, which was the new name for the Petty Officers' mess. The ship's company had taken cheerfully to the idea of their unusual passengers: it would mean overcrowding in spaces which were already used to the limit, but it would also be something new, a change, and therefore pleasing. Patrols were all too frequently uneventful, three weeks of discomfort and uninteresting food, and when days and weeks went by without a sight of an enemy – or at any rate, without a shot at one – well, you could get sick of it. But this time, they'd a U-boat to their credit already, and soon they'd have a bishop and a pack of women too. *That*'d be something to tell the lads about, when they got back!

Wyllie, there, would have another lot of stitching to do, before they got into harbour. A new red bar for a warship sunk, and a white dagger for a special operation – those emblems would have to be sewn on to the already well-adorned Jolly Roger. When you had a blank patrol, nothing to show for the weeks of waiting, you didn't fly the Roger when you came back. But when you'd made a killing, or killings, you flew it over the bridge, from a slightly raised periscope. It was the first thing the base staff and men from other submarines looked for when one of the flotilla was getting in from patrol. It was something to be proud of, that black flag with its central skull and crossbones: a record of achievements. Entering harbour, men in the bridge and on the casing would glance up, now and then, just for the pleasure of seeing it flapping there.

Olsen moved to the after periscope, and flicked his fingers. It was smaller than the other, and had no magnification; the top of it, the part that showed above the water and held the upper lens, was very much thinner than the other one. With the sea as smooth as it was today, so that any speck of white would be visible for miles, it was safer to take a preliminary look through this one and then have a more thorough search with the big fellow when you'd already made sure there was nothing close, no aircraft overhead.

Nothing. He folded the handles up and stepped over to the for'ard periscope; the E.R.A. had one of them shooting down and the other rising. Olsen grabbed the handles and swivelled slowly round, determined that if there was anything to see, he'd see it. In a few minutes — it was getting on for six thirty – Soames would be along to take over, and if a man taking over a watch found something in his first search, well, there was always a feeling that it had been there all the time and the other man had missed it.

But the sea was empty, and the sky a pale grey-blue without a speck in it.

Olsen murmured, 'Down periscope,' and turned to check the trim. That was another possible humiliation; if you were lazy, and let the 'planesmen work to keep the boat at her ordered depth when in fact she was a bit heavy for'ard, or light aft, matters which you could adjust easily enough to set things right, and then the new man as soon as he took over had a couple of gallons pumped out of the for'ard internal tank so that the 'planesmen could take the angle off and relax – then, they were liable to look at the chap who'd taken over, and think 'Ah – *this* bloke knows his onions, anyway!'

But the trim was perfect. *Setter* was going slow ahead on only one motor: the 'planes were horizontal and the depth was exactly right. Olsen had adjusted things after the watchkeepers changed over at six o'clock, when the move-round of weights of different men on duty had upset the delicate balance. Now, there was nothing more to do.

He looked at his watch: six twenty-seven. Soames should be here, by now. Olsen was hungry, and he wanted his breakfast; he'd developed a surprising taste for Soya Links and for *Setter*'s peculiar brand of coffee.

.   .   .   .

'You'd better read these notes, Olsen.' MacGregor stretched across the wardroom table, handing him some typed sheets of quarto paper. This had been Soames's work, last night; Olsen could see at once what he'd meant about the ribbon. The Captain said, 'Orders for the reception of your Norwegian friends. *Our* Norwegian friends. Incidentally, this is where you start earning your keep, my lad.'

'Earning keep?'

' 'M. You're the Liaison Officer. You're responsible for the passengers' welfare, comfort, entertainment. Who knows – the girl may be pretty!'

Chief muttered, 'If she is – *Sir* – I know who'll be doing most of the entertaining, if that's the word for it nowadays.'

'If I had any idea what you meant, Massingbird, I might construe that as insubordination. But fortunately, I haven't.'

Crawshaw shook his head. 'She won't be pretty. If I know *my* luck, she'll look more like the back end of a cart-horse.'

'*Your* luck?' Chief stared rudely at the First Lieutenant.

'Where d'you think *you* come into it?'

Crawshaw smiled. 'You're married, Chief, aren't you? 'M. And you, Sir – wasn't that an engagement in the paper, last time in? Yes, I thought it was. Well, that leaves me as senior unattached officer.'

'I hate to depress you all,' said the Captain. 'But I think I should point out before you get too excited that this girl may be eleven years old. Or three.'

Chief jerked a thumb at Crawshaw. 'Eleven'd be all right for *this* bugger.'

'That'll cost you sixpence, Chief.' Crawshaw held out the empty cigarette tin which was the wardroom swear-box.

'I haven't got one.'

'Then sign an I.O.U.'

MacGregor turned back to Olsen. 'As I was saying, you're Liaison Officer. Your job's to keep 'em all happy; that's what we've got you for, after all.' Olsen nodded, and the Captain went on, 'And one of the first things you've got to do is to show each one of them how to blow the heads and make sure they catch on. I don't want the things jammed all the time, and it'll be much less embarassing for our guests – 'specially the women – to have it explained right from the start, rather than someone having to go in there and do it for them every time one of them has a –' MacGregor paused. 'Nearly lost sixpence . . . I mean, every time.'

Olsen thought, that's a charming job – demonstrating to a bishop and his womenfolk how to pull the chain! But of course, MacGregor was right. They'd have to be shown, and he could do it in Norwegian much better than any of the others could do it in English. Crawshaw, for instance: when anyone failed to understand him, all he did was to repeat the sentence louder and more loudly still until he was almost shouting. Olsen smiled to himself as he pictured the unfortunate bishop, stuck in the tiny lavatory with Crawshaw screaming frantically in his ear . . .

Blowing the heads was a complicated business for the uninitiated. You had to open a valve to build up a reserve of air pressure in the cylinder, watching a gauge to get that pressure just right. Then open the outside valve – a most important move, that – push a lever over, pause, pull it back again, then turn another valve-wheel to let the charge of air whumph in and blow everything out into the sea. The pressure had to be big enough to overcome the external pressure of the sea, and that of course varied according to the depth of the submarine.

If you failed to open the external valve, the hull outlet, and then you went ahead with the other operations and finally sent the high-pressure in, you got what was known as a flash-back. It all came back, as powerfully as if it had been fired out of a cannon. As the closet was very small, and as you had to be leaning over the pan to operate the mechanism, you could hardly avoid getting it between the eyes.

Not a very suitable predicament for the wife of a bishop; and Olsen thought, if it should happen, I will be held responsible . . .

He told the Captain, 'I will write down the instructions, in Norwegian, and put this in the heads, in case they can forget the things I tell them.'

'Olsen, that's an absolutely first class idea! Do it now – here –' he flipped a signal pad across the table, and Crawshaw gave him a stout blue pencil, and he set to work. He put it down in numbered items, all very clearly and in short, simple words, bearing in mind that the daughter *might*, as MacGregor had suggested, be eleven years old. When he'd finished, he took the sheet of paper into the heads, which were on the starboard side, opposite the galley.

Ellis was flipping a cloth over the table, for breakfast, when he came back. Olsen squeezed into the gap between the table and the bench which separated it from Chief's bunk, and told them all. 'There is no place to put it except in the paper-box. Please, if you would be careful not to –'

'All right, Olsen, all right. I'm allergic to blue pencil, anyway . . . Soya Links again, Ellis?'

Ellis nodded. He wasn't going to let these —ers make him talk. After his money they were, same as that —ing Cox'n, who'd just bumped into him in the gangway when he was carrying a kettle of boiling water, and then, after listening appreciatively for about half a minute, robbed him of two-and-sixpence.

Soames's voice, from the Control Room: 'Captain, Sir!' Muttering under his breath, MacGregor tore himself away from the smell of *ersatz* sausages (skinless, made largely out of Soya beans, canned in white and unidentifiable fat) and shot into the Control Room.

'Eh?'

'Aircraft, Sir. Seaplane again. Green one-three-oh, angle of sight five, moving right to left. You can see him through this one.' Soames was standing by the after periscope, which he'd just lowered.

MacGregor took a look. 'Where the hell . . . oh, yes . . . ' He swivelled round, all the way, his feet moving in a blind and practised manner around the rim of the periscope well. Then he settled again on the seaplane. 'Looks like it's just patrolling. Routine, I expect . . . ' He said it, but he didn't think so. He nodded to the E.R.A., who sent the brass tube hissing back into its well.

'Stick to the after periscope, Sub, and keep an eye on that bugger. Keep a note of times it's in sight, and if it *is* patrolling I dare say you'll see it alter course. Let me know if it turns towards or comes any closer. Don't use the for'ard periscope at all. All right?'

'Aye aye, Sir. Er – sixpence, Sir.'

'What's that?'

'In the box, Sir.' Soames pointed to it. It was against the W/T office bulkhead, on top of the demolition charge. 'You referred to the aircraft with a prohibited word, Sir.'

The men in the Control Room were watching the Captain, and grinning at him; he went into the wardroom and got a coin out of his personal drawer, came back and dropped it in the box. It fell on other coins. Soames had the periscope up again, by that time; with his eyes at the lenses he told the Captain, 'It's turning, Sir. Towards.'

MacGregor took over the periscope. After a moment he muttered, 'It's going back the other way. It's an A/S patrol, all right by the looks of it.' He stepped back into the wardroom for his breakfast.

It was odd, he thought, the Germans having that patrol out. They knew perfectly well that British submarines didn't operate in these latitudes in midsummer. So why have planes up looking for them?

There were two possible answers, the first of them highly unpalatable. This one, the nasty thought that didn't bear thinking about – but which had to be faced and reckoned with – was that the enemy had news of something cooking. If this was the truth of it, there were two unpleasant sides to the situation: one, *Setter* could be moving into a trap when she made her run-in to the coast, and two, what chance did the bishop's party stand? But the other possible solution, and the one which MacGregor greatly preferred, was that there was some important ship, or even convoy, on the move, and that it was sufficiently important for Jerry to be taking every possible precaution in protecting it. This was in fact a not unlikely theory; and if *Setter* had been on an ordinary patrol MacGregor would have felt like nipping in a bit closer in the hope of finding a target for torpedoes. There might be a great, fat transport, lolloping up the coast, just asking to be sunk . . .

But – damn it! – if there was a convoy, it would be doing just that, hugging the coast. So why would there be an air patrol this far out?

.   .   .   .

The plane stayed there, limping up and down like a tired mosquito, close to the horizon. It'd be almost out of sight to the north, then Soames would see the light on its wings as it banked and turned, and it'd go back over its course again until it was just a speck on the submarine's starboard quarter. A set and steady patrol.

Just before Crawshaw took over from Soames at eight-thirty, a second plane appeared. For about ten minutes they were both in sight, then the first one turned away towards Norway and flew into the horizon. The new one – a seaplane like the first – kept up the same monotonous up-and-down routine.

MacGregor came to the conclusion that they were gaining nothing by watching the aircraft, and only taking a risk, however slight it was at this range, of being spotted. He sent the periscope down and told Crawshaw, who was there ready to take over the watch, 'Sixty feet, Number One.'

'Sixty feet, Sir.'

Setter ambled down to the safe, quiet depth, and Crawshaw pumped water out of the two midships tanks to adjust her trim to the higher density. When he'd got it right, she was as steady as a rock.

MacGregor lay in his bunk, thinking about the air search. It made no odds now – whatever its purpose – but he didn't like the indications or the feel of the situation. Even if all this activity was quite unconnected with *Setter*, it was worrying, and if it kept up it was going to make the run-in extremely difficult if not downright impossible. They'd a longish way to go, to the rendezvous postion, and to get there on time they'd have to do most of the distance on the surface. Eight hours, it would need, at the submarine's maximum speed. If the planes kept them down, or put them down after they'd surfaced, for any length of time, then they'd miss the appointment. Then the bishop and his party would be in an extremely hazardous position and *Setter* herself might be in trouble.

MacGregor sat up, stuck his legs over the side of the bunk, and slid down. He went to the chart table, and made a quick calculation of their present Dead Reckoning position, and marked it on the chart. Then he closed his eyes for greater concentration while he estimated the range of the patrolling aircraft and the length of their patrol line; he marked that, too, on the chart, and it looked to him to be reasonably accurate. He decided that if he put *Setter* to slow ahead on both motors, instead of just on one, that'd give her a reasonable three knots instead of something under two which was her present speed by the log. He took the parallel rulers and laid out first a course to clear the end of the seaplane's patrol line, then a new one from that point which would take them in directly towards the rendezvous. He ran the rulers to the compass rose in the corner of the chart, and noted both courses in the navigational notebook; then, with dividers, he measured the run to the point of changing course; he thought, three knots . . . he closed his eyes again and got the answer pat, four hours and fifteen minutes. That would make it thirteen hundred hours: 1 pm., to alter course from 010 degrees, to 090. He noted it in the book, and called to Crawshaw.

'Number One.'

'Sir?'

'Go slow ahead together, and come round to oh-one-oh.'

'Aye aye, Sir . . . Slow ahead together. Starboard ten.'

The bell rang on the telegraph as the messenger whirled the brass handle, and the helmsman repeated, 'Steer oh-one-oh, Sir!' MacGregor leant over the chart table again, checking his courses and distances. He heard Crawshaw tell the fore 'planesmen, 'Keep her down!'

The application of rudder and the turning movement made the bow tend to rise, and the for'ard hydroplanes needed some angle of dive on them to correct that. If the man had been properly alert, he'd have put some on at the same moment as the helmsman spun his wheel.

It was easy to be sleepy, at sixty feet. Nothing to worry about, nothing to do except watch a depth-gauge; it was warm in the Control Room, and the hum of the motors was almost inaudible.

The only noticeable sounds were the ticking of the electric log and the scraping sound as the Asdic operator trained his intrument, turning the pointer that moved the oscillator which was now not transmitting Asdic impulses but acting as a hydrophone: if a surface ship (or, for that matter, a submarine) came within miles, he'd hear its screws churning the sea. H.E., that was called, or Hydrophone Effect, and if you knew what sort of a ship it was you could get its approximate speed by counting those audible revolutions of its propellors and checking them against the hand of a stopwatch.

But the operator's face was blank, bored, his eyes as expressionless as those of a cow chewing the cud. Only his fingers moved – long, bony fingers, the backs of them covered with thick, black hair – as he twisted the dial a degree or two at a time, pausing and listening then turning it again, all around the compass and for two hours on end.

The helmsman reported the new course, and Crawshaw told the Captain, 'Course oh-one-oh, Sir.'

'Very good. We alter to oh-nine-oh at one o'clock.'

Crawshaw nodded. MacGregor glanced round the Control Room again, taking in the boredom, the placid stillness of the routine. The ticking of the log only emphsized the silence. He thought, this time tomorrow – we'll be on our toes!

But now — there wasn't anything to do but wait.

9

STOKER Sluggs Martin, like several others, decided that while the submarine was dived, quiet and level, this would be an excellent time to shave the bristles off his face. It was a very strange idea, this shaving in the middle of a patrol, but the Captain had said they had to, and Sluggs had no doubt that anyone who didn't do it would get into serious and immediate trouble.

Mac was an easy-going bloke, always ready for a pint of wallop if you met him ashore, but he could be a bloody terror when he was angry and the quickest way to find that out was to ignore an order. It had been tried once or twice, in the early days of the comission, but nobody tried it any more.

Well, if you were going to shave, this was the time, with

the boat steady as a rock; moreover, there'd be a queue for the basin later on, when everyone else suddenly thought of it. The stokers lived in the After Ends – the tail of the submarine – and there was only one stainless steel washbowl for all of them. At the moment, Knocker Wilson was in possession, studiously lathering his broad, full cheeks.

' 'Ere, Knocker. I'm next after you with that basin, see?'

Knocker wiped soap from his lips, and nodded. 'All right with me, mate. Soon's I'm done, you can do what you —ing well like in it, f' all I care.'

'Cost you a tanner, that will, Knocker.'

Knocker Wilson jerked in surprise, cut his cheek, and swore again. Martin laughed.

'And that makes a bob, mate.' He routed out his shaving gear, and found there was no blade in the razor. He was opening his mouth to ask Knocker for the loan of one, when he remembered that he'd lent his own to Able Seaman Hughes, more generally known as Lofty, the night before they left Dundee. Well, now he'd get it back, and quick. 'I'm off for'ard a minute, mate. 'Ang on to that basin till I'm back, will you?' Knocker, scowling furiously at his own image in the stained mirror, didn't answer.

Martin went for'ard, wearing a small towel wrapped around his waist. He stopped in the Control Room, and asked the First Lieutenant, who had the afternoon watch – it was getting on for four o'clock – 'Permission to go for'ard, Sir?'

Crawshaw glanced round, and nodded. Men off watch had to ask permission to go from one end of the boat to the other, when she was dived; if too many moved around at once, it could play hell with the trim. *Setter* was back at periscope depth, now; they'd come up for a look round soon after altering course at one o'clock, and as there'd been no sign of any aircraft they'd stayed there.

Martin went on, past the wardroom, the galley, the Ladies' Boudoir, the E.R.A.'s mess and the Leading Sea-Seamen's mess, into the Fore Ends. It was a dim cavern, hammocks slung overhead obliterating most of the light which came from fixed bulbs on the deckhead. He bent double, and picked his way carefully through the compartment, taking care not to tread on men whose bedding was spread on the deck itself. Fortunately, Lofty Hughes was awake, and made very little fuss before he handed over the small, blue blade.

Martin inspected it closely. 'You might've —ing well wiped it, mate!'

Hughes shrugged, missing or ignoring the sixpenny-worth. 'Weren't worth it. You couldn't cut y' finger on it, no matter 'ow 'ard you tried. Blunt, see? You'll not do much with it, Sluggs, not with that one.'

Martin started aft, muttering angrily to himself. It had been a new blade, almost, plenty of life left in it, when that bloody Welshman cadged it. Sluggs was examining it as he padded along on his bare feet, trying to scrape the solidi-fied soap-and-bristle crustation off its edge with his thumb nail, and thinking that if he stropped it on the edge of his hand it might see him through just one shave. Preoccupied with this, he didn't see the Stoker Petty Officer, Harms-worth, ahead of him in the gangway until he practically knocked him down.

'Where the 'ell you off to, Martin?'

'Aft. 'Xcuse me –'

'Martin: didn't you 'ear the Captain, this morning? Cover y'self up!'

Sluggs looked down at the disarranged towel. 'Oh. *This*, you mean?'

The Petty Officer's features twisted in disgust. 'What an 'orrible thing! Fancy carryin' a nasty looking object like that round with you, all the days of y' life!'

Martin returned his stare. 'I don't *carry* it, Stokes, I *follers* it. An' it takes me into some —ing interesting situations, I don't mind tellin' you . . . 'Xcuse me, now.' He pushed by, heading aft.

''Ang on, there. I've not finished with you, not by a long chalk . . .' Martin stopped, and turned back. The Stoker P.O. ticked points off on his fingers: 'One, exposin' y'self – that's a tanner. Two, loose talk – double it. Three, use of the word — , add a tanner. That's one-an'-six, an' I'll 'ave it *now*.'

Martin closed his eyes and pressed his lips together, thus suppressing a flow of language which would have cost him all of five shillings. When the pressure had eased, he told the Stoker P.O., 'All right. I'll bring it when I've completed me *toilette* which is French for a chamfer-up, as you might not 'ave known. Now, Petty Officer 'Armsworth, if you'll pardon me, I'll –' he was going to say, ' — off', but once again he forced his lips together and paused. He finished, 'I'll proceed upon me way aft.' He raised his right hand, finger and thumb forming a circle through which he gazed haughtily, as though through a lorgnette, at Harmsworth. Then with a disdainful sniff he turned and headed back towards the After Ends.

In the galley, Ellis was brewing tea and cutting thick slices of bread. Martin stopped, curtsied to him, holding the towel out sideways in an attitude of great delicacy. Ellis said, 'Charmed, I'm sure,' and Martin simpered archly before he moved on aft.

MacGregor and Olsen were sitting at the wardroom table, waiting for their tea; Soames and the engineer were asleep still, the curtains drawn across their bunks. Mac-Gregor glanced up as Martin padded by.

'Martin!'

'Sir?'

'You won't go around in that state when our passengers are on board. If the bishop's wife sticks her neck out of there –' he jerked a thumb in the direction of the Ladies' Boudoir – 'and she sees something like you, she'll have a stroke.'

Martin nodded. 'Aye aye, Sir.' As he went on into the Control Room, they heard him mutter, 'I'll stroke her, any time she likes . . .'

MacGregor laughed. Then he turned to the Norwegian. 'Look, Olsen. When we meet this fishing boat, since you're not only torpedo officer and gunnery officer but also casing officer, boarding officer and liaison officer, it'll be your job to get 'em aboard . . . You won't need all the casing party: I should think you, the Second Cox'n, and one other hand. 'M?'

Olsen nodded.

'You'll have to work fast. We'll be approaching the fishing boat dived, and when I'm sure there aren't any aircraft about we'll surface fast, the same as for gun action. You'll follow me up the hatch, and go over the side of the bridge, and your two men'll use the guntower hatch. That'll save time, and it'll be easier for the women than having to climb all the way up.'

MacGregor pondered, watching Ellis absent-mindedly as the messman brought in bread and butter, jam and Marmite, sugar, a jug of tinned milk, plates and knives. The Captain murmured, his thoughts still on women and climbing ladders, 'I hope they'll be wearing trousers.' Ellis glanced sharply at him: it was obvious that if there was a vote for it, he'd plump for skirts. He went back into the galley to get the tea.

'Well. I want you to work like greased lightning, Olsen. I'll surface as close as I safely can to the boat, and at an angle so that all they have to do is to give a touch ahead on their engine to come alongside the fore casing.' He paused, thinking it out. 'Get their boat abreast the gun, or just for'ard of it, so they won't have far to go: out of the boat, up on the casing, straight into the hatch. No hanging around. Soon as the last of them's in the hatch, your two men and then you, and you shut and clamp it prontissimo because by that time I'll have got clear of their boat and I'll be diving straight away; you won't get any warning. All right?'

'Yes. If the sea stays like it is today, it'll be easy, I think.'

'Perhaps. But you know, even now there's a bit of a swell, and although you hardly notice it when you're on your own, as we are now, the minute you put a boat alongside you bloody well *do*. Might be banging up and down quite a lot. Don't expect it to be *too* easy – especially with an old man and two women – or you'll get caught on the wrong foot.'

Olsen nodded. He was pretty new to submarines, but, he thought, I'm not *that* green. I doubt if I've any less sea-time to my credit than this fellow.

MacGregor must have been a mind-reader. 'Were you at sea before the war, Olsen?'

Startled, Olsen looked up quickly. 'Since I was a little boy. My father was Master of a tanker, and I sailed with him when I was – ' he held out his hand, palm down, at about the level of the table-top. 'Altogether I have been more time at sea than in Norway.'

MacGregor looked at him with a certain respect, the

look of one professional for another. Ellis was bringing in the tea.

'Better shake that body, Sub.' Olsen leant down and pulled back Chief's curtains, then banged on the engineer's shoulder with the flat of his hand. The body rolled over, its face split by a yawn, so that a surprising gap showed pinkly between beard and moustache. Olsen slid along the bench, and roused Soames in the same way. While they were climbing out of their bunks, grumbling and stretching, MacGregor opened a new subject with the Norwegian. Perhaps he'd been working up to it all along.

'You were in *Virulent*, weren't you, before they sent you up to Lerwick?'

'Yes.'

' 'M. Off to the Med. I dare say you'll want to rejoin her, after this jaunt?'

'Will they not keep me in Lerwick?'

'Oh, no. You were only sent there for us. But – well, you see, Henning – the chap whose place you took – he's due to get a First Lieutenant's job at any moment. In fact this would've been his last patrol with me. So – I'll be needing a new Sub-Lieutenant. If you'd like the idea, I could ask for you to be appointed.'

'Well, thank you –'

'I'd understand perfectly if you wanted to go back to *Virulent*. She's sailed by now, but I dare say they'll let you take passage to Malta as an extra watchkeeper in some other boat. Anyway, think it over.'

'I would like to stay in *Setter*, Sir.'

MacGregor looked pleased. 'Well, that's fine. Anyway, you can change your mind if you want to – you've got until we get back before I can do anything about it. But if you still want to then, I can certainly fix it ... what's the matter with *you*, Chief?'

The engineer had put his cup down with an expression indicating nausea. 'If there was somewhere I could spit ... In *real* ships, they use this sort of liquid for polishing brass with.' He looked at Olsen. 'I'd take the chance of going back to what's-its-name, if I were you. Before you get bloody well poisoned.'

Tea was about finished, and Olsen was thinking it was time he went to take over the watch, when Crawshaw's voice, raised in sudden excitement, called, 'Captain, Sir!'

MacGregor slid out, wiping his mouth on the back of his hand as he went. He found Crawshaw with the small periscope raised. As MacGregor came into the Control Room, the First Lieutenant flicked up the handles and told the E.R.A., 'Dip.' The man depressed his lever; the periscope dropped six feet or so, then he checked it and brought it slowly up again, into the Captain's hands. Crawshaw said, 'Smoke, Sir. Green one-oh.'

MacGregor peered into the lenses. He muttered, 'Smoke it is, indeed.' He swivelled round fast, then pushed the handles up and stepped over to the larger periscope, the for'ard one. As it hissed up out of its well he was thinking, perhaps this will explain the air search, those seaplanes. A convoy – or a capital ship making a run for the Atlantic! If it was that, he'd be in a bit of a quandary; now, of all times, *Setter* had to keep out of sight, get in to that rendezvous quietly, quickly and unseen. But apart from the orders for this particular operation, *Setter* (and every other unit in the Royal Navy, as well) was under permanent and overriding orders which were never in eclipse so long as Britain was at war: to 'seek out and destroy the enemy, wherever he may be found ... '

You didn't achieve that end by going deep and pretending to be an ostrich. It had been reported that certain Italian submarines, in the Mediterranean, had spent the duration of their patrols lying on the bottom and then fired their torpedoes into empty wastes of sea before returning to their bases with stories of hazard and heroism for which they were awarded medals: but neither *Setter* nor her crew was Italian.

Through the big periscope, with the magnification in, MacGregor saw the smoke more clearly; it was, as Crawshaw had said, fine on the starboard bow.

'Down periscope. Diving Stations.'

While men rushed past to take over their action positions, some of them still chewing, or half dressed – the Cox'n, for instance, had shaved exactly half his face and the left side of it was still lathered – MacGregor called for the periscope again. The E.R.A. of the watch started it on its way up, but by the time it was raised Featherstone had taken over the job, and it was he who stopped it. Quickly, MacGregor swept all round the sky and horizon; then settled on the smoke. He trained left, and studied a second smoke-plume which he'd noticed, briefly, in the course of the more rapid search. So it was a convoy, by the looks of it . . . Back on the right-hand smudge, he caught a first glimpse of a slender masthead and crosstrees.

Hutchins, the Asdic operator, spoke up sharply. 'H.E., Sir, Green one-two. Second lot, Red two-two.'

'What's it sound like, Hutchins?'

'Reciprocating engine. Frigates, could be –'

'Up periscope . . . Keep her down, Number One. Thirty two feet.' He grabbed the handles, and stooped to the lenses. Top of a funnel, now, and a bit of bridge superstructure. Grey-black. That's the one to the right. Now on

85

the other . . . yes, two of the same class, anti-submarine trawlers. Come into my parlour: and *Setter* was the fly, complying all too readily with the unspoken invitation. So now they knew the worst, he thought: it *was Setter* they were after, and God help the bishop, because it didn't look very much as if they'd be able to do much about that end of things. Not unless they were incredibly lucky. The time for wishful thinking was past and gone; following on the aircraft, this would be too much of a coincidence for any other explanation to fit.

'Flood Q – a hundred and fifty feet!'

Featherstone jerked back the lever which opened the Kingston flood-valve on 'Q' quick-diving tank; at the same moment the after 'planesman swung his wheel to angle the submarine downwards, and the other man on the for'ard 'planes put his to dive. *Setter*'s bow went down and she sank fast, the needles travelling rapidly round the depth-gauges.

'When you've got it buttoned, Number One, stop the port motor.'

'Aye aye, Sir.' Crawshaw had the ballast pump working on the port and starboard midships tanks. At a hundred feet he told Featherstone, 'Blow "Q".'

'Blow Q, Sir.' The E.R.A. had already slammed Q Kingston shut; now he opened the H.P. air valve to blow the water out of the tank. The submarine was dropping like a stone into deep water, and the aim was now to level her off at a hundred and fifty feet, and to stop her getting out of control and going on deeper. The farther down you got, the harder it was to come out of the dive; as she went down, she got heavier, and the momentum of the descent increased. Submarines of *Setter*'s class were tested to three hundred and fifty feet, and although some of them had been down much deeper, her builders weren't responsible for what might happen at any greater depth than that.

(Anyone – everyone – knew what *might* happen. If you took an egg in the palm of your hand and squeezed until it smashed – that was roughly the picture.)

MacGregor's plan was to stay on this course, and pass at depth and as slowly – therefore as quietly – as possible between the two hunting craft on the surface. There were several good reasons for such a course. First, if *Setter* turned away from the enemy she'd give their Asdics a much bigger target: they'd have the full length of the submarine to pick up, instead of the comparatively small bows-on silhouette. Second, *Setter* had to get inshore of them in any case; so if she escaped seaward now she'd still have to get in past them later on, if she was going to keep her appointment with the bishop. Third – and if you needed any more reasons for an automatic decision which under these circumstances was the only right one – to turn away and escape surface ships which were steaming towards her and travelling faster than her own maximum speed submerged, the only way to do it would have been to get away at right angles to their own course, and at high revolutions, full ahead on both motors, thus making so much propeller noise that they'd have to be either drunk or dead, up there, to fail to hear her.

Crawshaw got *Setter* out of her nosedive at a hundred and sixty feet, and the 'planesmen brought her back up to the one-fifty mark, the ordered depth. A moment later the trim seemed right, or close enough, to be able to hold that depth at a lower speed. He told the messenger, 'Stop port.'

MacGregor asked Hutchins, 'H.E. bearings now?'

Hutchins fiddled with the Asdic dial, his eyes half

closed as he concentrated on the sounds which came to him out of the headphones. He told the Captain, 'Green two-five, Sir. And . . . Red one-six.'

'You sure of that?' If Hutchins was right, the one on the port bow had closed in. It meant that instead of passing between the two trawlers, at these relative courses and speeds that one on the port bow was going to pass ahead of the submarine.

Hutchins nodded. 'Positive, Sir . . . Transmitting, both of 'em.'

Well, *of course* they'd be transmitting. An A/S trawler wasn't much use if it didn't. The only thing was, would their transmissions find *Setter*? If they did – but Mac-Gregor thought, there's every chance they won't. With any luck, they're half asleep . . .

Hutchins reported, 'That bearing's steady, Sir. Red one-six, closing.'

A steady bearing meant that she wasn't going to pass either ahead or astern of *Setter*. She was going slap over the top. MacGregor watched Hutchins as he twiddled the dial and concentrated through his ears. Crawshaw watched the trim: he stood behind and between the two 'planesmen, with his back against the steel ladder which led to the hatch: he watched the needles in the depth-gauges and the angles on the hydroplane indicators and the level of the bubble in the long, curved spirit-level. The helmsman, turning his wheel a little this way and that to keep the submarine on her course, watched the pointer against the card of the gyro compass.

The 'planesmen watched their depth-gauges. Soames, leaning over the chart table, fiddled with a pencil and listened to the orders and reports from the Control Room. Olsen stood by the Fruit Machine, watching the Captain.

Featherstone watched him, too, and so did the messenger and the signalman. Nobody moved, except to do his immediate job, and nobody spoke; silence added to the growing tension in the Control Room while each of them pictured, mentally, the scene on the surface as the two trawlers closed in on *Setter*'s track.

They, too, had Asdic operators: men like Hutchins here, only of course German. Like him, they'd be crouched over their sets, pushing the control dials round and listening to the sharp, high-pitched impulses singing out and fading into the ocean; hoping – even perhaps praying – for one of those transmissions to come echoing back into the headphones, bouncing off a submerged hull, the sudden and unexpected but always looked for reward for weeks and months of searching and patrolling, of discomfort, sea-sickness and utter boredom.

Hutchins moved, suddenly. His whole body stiffened and his Adam's apple wobbled furiously and he told Mac-Gregor,

'They're in contact, Sir. Red one-oh, closing, in contact: Green four-oh, stopped, in contact.'

MacGregor snapped, 'Two hundred feet – port twenty! Half ahead together. Shut off for depth-charging!'

10

THE bicycle had been made to be ridden by women; there was no crossbar and the machine was of an old-fashioned shape, high off the ground, with tall, prim handlebars. The back wheel had a fan of strings on it, once coloured but now bleached and many of them missing; they stretched from hub to mudguard and their purpose, of course, had been to keep the hems of skirts from becoming entangled in the spokes. Being old, the machine rattled, and its natural instincts combined with the decrepitude engendered by years of hard use made it resist Kjellegard's efforts to drive it along at a speed inconsistent with its own notions of prudence and decorum: whenever it reached such a speed that he could actually feel the wind passing his ears, its rusty chain slipped off the cogs between the pedals, so that he had to stop, dismount, and with difficulty re-rig the ancient and reluctant driving-mechanism. On one such occasion the chain had managed to trap his forefinger against the sharp, worn cog-wheel, and now his left hand's dirt was streaked with blood.

The air was cool, but he sweated as he drove along, the sharp prow of the saddle causing him continuous and maddening discomfort, and the urgency in his mind provided an inner disturbance which aggravated and inflamed the physical strains and effort.

It would have been forty miles if he'd taken the direct route, and that, God knew, would have been more than far enough when every single minute counted: the message had to get to London, so that from that distant hub of freedom the news of a change in plans could be relayed to the submarine in time to divert her from the original rendezvous. The signal to her from London must get to her tonight: at latest, Kjellegard thought, by midnight. If it didn't reach her in time to turn her back, she'd be spending this night closing in to a pointless and possibly dangerous rendezvous. By the fact that the Germans had descended on the little fishing port, concentrated their first searches on the wharf and immediate area of the harbour, and arresting those two men as casually as if they'd been expecting to find them just there, it was pretty obvious that there'd been a leak. *How much* had leaked: that was the question! If they knew about the submarine, and the message didn't get through in time for her to be stopped and turned back, and the Germans were waiting for her – well, she'd be in trouble, and as a consequence of that the odds were that there'd be no second rendezvous because there'd be no submarine to keep it. And that would mean disaster for the Dalens: with the Germans so close on their heels, if they didn't get out within a day or two they never would.

Kjellegard grinned painfully to himself as he saw the final oddity of the situation. So many lives, a British ship, and a man who was loved from one end of Norway to the other – all of these depended entirely on this frightful old rattletrap of a bicycle.

He hadn't taken the direct route. For all the urgency, it would have been much too dangerous to have risked being caught cycling inland from that point on the coast which was at the moment a centre of so much Gestapo interest. The road would very likely be patrolled, and even if it wasn't, a chance encounter could be fatal. You could fool a lot of the Germans most of the time, when you knew the ropes and had the answers and the right sets of forged papers ready; but when it was the Gestapo you were dealing with, and when they had a clear scent in their nostrils and a quarry so close ahead that they could almost taste its blood – well, only a fool would take chances . . . So he'd cut down in a south-easterly direction until he'd got to a crossroads so that he could turn up to the left and be ready with a story of having started his journey on the other side of Trondheim. One of the sets of papers which he carried would confirm that that was where he worked. He was a sailmaker, and the reason for his present journey was that his old mother was seriously ill: he had her letter in his pocket, a shaky, old woman's spindly script, smudged and misspelt. It was so obviously authentic that no German would guess it had been written early that day, by Anna at his dictation, and back-dated by a week, this to support his story that it had reached him by hand of a second cousin, a lad of twelve, who'd come all the way on foot with the letter inside his shirt where the old woman, reaching out of her bed, with trembling hands, had pinned it.

Oh, he was a simple, gabby sailmaker, and he'd give them so many intimate family details that he'd bore their very ears off!

He leant his weight forward, thrusting down on the pedals, forcing the bicycle up to the top of a long rise which steepened suddenly just short of the top. His legs plunged like pistons and with each thrust the breath jerked out in grunts, and in his mind the count ran on; ninety-one, ninety-two, ninety-three. He was never aware of starting to count, but often found himself among the high numbers, hundred-and-one, hundred-and-two – he'd stop it angrily, and five minutes later he'd find that he was back in the eighties.

The top of the rise: his right foot went down hard as he breasted it, and at once a familiar absence of resistance combined with a clicking, rattling noise told him that the chain had come adrift again. But the machine was free-wheeling now, and the road fell away in front for a mile or more; he'd rest, let gravity do the work, and fix the chain at the bottom of the slope.

He was doing that, ten minutes later, when he heard the lorry's engine. Looking back the way he'd come, he saw its cab rising over the top of the hill.

There was no cover: not even a bank, or a ditch. In any

case, the driver would have seen him, by now. He knelt beside the bicycle and fiddled with its chain as the lorry hurtled towards him. He saw with relief that it was a civilian truck, and that there was only the driver in its cab.

The lorry was slowing, and as it came closer he saw that it was at least as old as the bicycle. The front mudguards flapped like elephants' ears and at this shorter distance there was more noise of rattling than of motor. It stopped beside him in a cloud of dust and a stink of overheated engine, and the driver opened the nearside door and stared down at him. He was a Norwegian, poorly dressed and badly in need of a haircut. A man of about sixty.

'Having trouble?'

'The chain comes off every ten metres. It's my sister's machine, damn her!'

'Chuck it in the back, man. If you're going my way?'

.   .   .   .

The church was at the end of the village, on a bit of a rise. Kjellegard had got out of the lorry near some farm cottages, which straggled out to the south of the village proper; he'd taken care to give the driver the impression that one of these hovels was his destination, and now he stood on the roadside until the lorry had gone on through, out past the church and over the rise, out of sight. When it was gone, he left the road, and more carrying than pushing the bicycle he set off across the fields to the right. Skirting the houses and farmyards, he came on to the church through the spinney on its eastern side; he left the bicycle there, among the trees, then knocked the worst of the dust out of his clothes and walked up to the back door of the rectory.

Pastor Iversen's wife caught her breath with surprise

when she saw him. She looked over his shoulder, down towards the village: then she told him, 'He's not here. Won't be long, perhaps, but I'm not sure.'

'I'll wait in the church. Please tell him it's urgent . . . You're well?'

'Yes, thank you. You?'

'Fine. How's the boy?'

She smiled, and cocked her head on one side. He heard the baby's voice: it was glugging, chortling to itself, somewhere inside the house.

'Well – if you'd be sure to tell him, please . . . '

The church door creaked, groaned as he pushed it open, and a smell of damp and woodrot met him as he stepped inside. Halfway up the short aisle, he slid into a pew. Now was the time to eat those sandwiches; he'd wanted to have them in the lorry, but the thought that he'd be obliged to offer some to the driver had deterred him. He'd be travelling again all night, and there was no prospect of any other food coming his way between now and tomorrow. He didn't want to take any from the Iversens, although he knew they'd have given him whatever they had, if he'd asked.

When he'd finished eating, he crumpled the paper and pushed it into his pocket. Then he lay out flat on the bench, using a dusty hassock as a pillow, and went to sleep.

It was the creak of the vestry door that woke him. Sitting up, he saw Iversen standing there just this side of it, peering shortsightedly into the gloom of the church. Kjellegard glanced at his watch; he'd been asleep for rather less than an hour. He stood up, wincing at the stiffness in his leg muscles. That damned bicycle – and he'd be on it again, in next to no time!

'Something's wrong? Our friend . . . ?'

'He's all right. Don't worry. Only – a message – *now*.' Kjellegard's eyes strayed upwards.

The priest nodded. 'Very well.' Kjellegard followed him into the vestry and up the narrow steps into the first floor of the wooden tower. It was no more than a loft, really. From here there was a ladder, a rickety thing, which led up higher; Kjellegard let the pastor get right up and out of sight before he put his own weight on the worn, thin rungs.

Iversen was already dragging aside the mountain of sacks and junk which hid the grey steel box of the transmitter. Plugging in the aerial, he told Kjellegard, 'You'd better write down what you want me to send. Make it as short as possible, please.'

Kjellegard flattened out the piece of paper in which his sandwiches had been wrapped. He found a stub of pencil in his pocket, and knelt on the floor, writing his message in block capitals and in English. When he'd finished, he read it through and crossed out one unnecessary word.

The set was warming up. Pastor Iversen took the message from Kjellegard, and opened a prayer book which looked at least fifty years old. Actually it had been put together in London, less than a year ago, and it contained the groups and keys to a simple code. Iversen coded the message quickly, using Kjellegard's blunt pencil to write the groups against each word on the greasy scrap of paper.

When he'd checked it, he put the square of paper on the top of the radio, which was humming strongly, ready to transmit. The pastor's fingers flicked the 'send-receive' switch to 'send', then moved swiftly to the morse transmitter key and began to tap out a call-sign.

Kjellegard sat on the floor, watching that pale, bony hand pecking like a hen at the dots and dashes. He was thinking, It's a hell of a long way round to have to send a message: to London, and back again to a submarine that's only about a hundred miles away from where I'm sitting . . .

II

THE watertight bulkhead doors between all the submarine's compartments had been shut, and so had various hull outlets and the smaller depth-gauges. In each compartment there were things to shut off, and now as *Setter* nosed down to two hundred feet and swung sharply to port at the same time as she increased speed, a man in each of the compartments reported by telephone to the Control Room, 'Tube Space shut off for depth-charging,' 'Engine room shut off for depth-charging' . . . When all the reports were in, Crawshaw told the Captain, 'All compartments shut off, Sir, communications tested.' He had that pump going again, to lighten the tanks at the new depth.

'Steer three-two-oh.'

'Steer three-two-oh, Sir.' The helmsman centred his wheel to ease the rate of turn. Crawshaw stopped the pump and said, 'Two hundred feet, Sir.'

'Very good . . . Slow together.'

'Slow ahead together, Sir.' Wyllie passed the order to the motor room by telephone: the telegraphs were disconnected, now, to cut out that unnecessary source of noise.

Hutchins reported, 'Enemy lost contact, Sir. H.E. bearings drawing right. Green five-oh, and Green nine-five.'

MacGregor's face brightened. It was a step in the right

direction, and a hopeful sign that just an alteration of course and a change of depth should have thrown the enemy off the scent. He said, happily, 'Stop starboard.'

If they could creep away, now, as silently as possible, paddle gently away to the north west while the enemy searched for them where they'd been before – well, in any direction but this one – creep away like a mouse sneaking through a room full of cats ...

'One's in contact, Sir. Green five-three.'

It had been too much to hope for. Smiles faded. The cat had looked the other way, but not for long.

'Both in contact, Sir ... Green five-three, stopped, other one Green nine-six, closing, H.E. increasing.'

So one of the trawlers was stopped, holding them in contact while the other made an attacking run. The joke was over, now, and play had begun in earnest. In the Control Room they could hear the Asdic pings, high, tiny sounds as they bounced off *Setter*'s hull, from there straight back to inform the enemy of the submarine's position.

'Group up, full ahead together! Starboard twenty; steer oh-four-oh.'

MacGregor stood leaning on the ladder in the centre of the Control Room; he had one foot on its bottom rung. Wyllie passed the order to the motor room and they felt the sudden power of the screws as the motors were put hard ahead, grouped up, which meant connected in parallel instead of in series, to get the full and simultaneous power of both batteries. (There were fifty-six cells in each of the two batteries, and each cell stood half the height of a man.) One of the trawlers was at this moment pounding in to drop charges, and MacGregor was hoping to get out of the line of attack by sudden speed and a change of course. At the same time, the burst of power from the screws would churn

97

up the water and leave a disturbance which could camouflage the submarine's movement and confuse those Asdic operators on the surface.

But the power of the batteries was a precious thing which had to be conserved, and you didn't stay grouped-up and full ahead for longer than necessary. You had to make sure that the battery lasted at least as long as the enemy stayed on the hunt, because when the power was exhausted you'd have to surface, and then you'd be at his mercy, which was something no enemy possessed.

'Group down. Half ahead together.'

Hutchins said, almost apologetically, 'Loud H.E., Sir, bearing slowly right.'

That spurt and change of course had served their immediate purpose: the trawler was coming in on a fixed course, based on an estimation of *Setter*'s last course and speed as calculated by the enemy's Asdic plot: that the bearing was drawing right meant that he'd been thrown off and would not, after all, be passing right overhead. But it didn't need Asdics now to hear the trawler; everyone in the submarine could hear her threshing propellers as she pounded down on their starboard side.

By now, depth-charges would have been dropped, and thrown, and they'd be on their way down, their firing pistols set to explode at a set depth . . .

The standard procedure for depth-charging was to drop them in patterns of five, the shape being that of a diamond with one in the middle for luck. As the enemy approached the spot which he had reckoned to be the submarine's position, he'd let one charge roll off the stern rack, and fire two others out of the throwers, one on each side of the ship. That made the bottom point of the diamond, and also the two outside ones – which, through the angle of the throwers and also because of the forward velocity of the ship, would be flung ahead as well as outwards. So the next charge to be dropped, the central one of the pattern, would be slipped out of the stern racks at about the same time as the last two, which had been thrown out and forwards, hit the water. Then the final charge, the fifth, would be dropped out of the stern racks, and there was the complete diamond, composed of five barrels of high explosive. It covered a wide area of sea and the enemy hoped that one of the five charges would explode close enough to the submarine to smash her, damage her, or force her to the surface.

'Group up, full ahead together!'

Again, *Setter* plunged forward, her deck and hull trembling under the power and vibration of the screws. MacGregor told the helmsman, 'Steer oh-three-oh.'

If charges had been dropped, when the trawler passed overhead, it was time they went off. Eyes tended to glance upwards, and even the most steady and unimaginative of *Setter*'s crew had mental pictures of those black canisters drifting down . . .

The sea erupted. *Setter* rang, as if she had been struck by some enormous hammer: she seemed to move bodily sideways, shaking from the giant blow: then she rolled, the other way, to starboard, the deck angling steeply as she was flung over twenty or thirty degrees, and the main lighting sputtered out. Emergency lights glowed weakly while the other charges, farther away but still frighteningly loud, echoed the blast and shock-waves of the first.

Setter was nose down, diving, the needles flying round the gauges; the planesmen were fighting to correct the angle but she was committed to the dive, as determined as a horse with the bit between its teeth . . . Crawshaw turned to

MacGregor. 'Slow, Sir; I can't –'

MacGregor snapped, 'Stop together. Group down.'

The screws slowed and stopped and she sank less fast. The gauges read three hundred feet, though, and she was still going down. Crawshaw could have pulled her up quickly enough by putting a puff of air into number one main ballast: but if he did that, he'd have to open the vent again to let the air out as soon as she was levelled off, and that would send an enormous bubble to the surface to tell the enemy exactly where she was. Instead, he had the ballast tank working on 'A', the for'ard internal tank.

Men were picking themselves up, and the lights came on again without warning: Olsen, who'd been flung off his feet and taken Featherstone with him in a fast slide across the deck which had been stopped only when they'd come up hard against the foot of the ladder, gingerly fingered a bruise on the top of his head. In passing, he'd cracked it against the steel rim around the well of the for'ard periscope. He said to the E.R.A., 'Sorry, I will remember to hold on, next time.'

Featherstone grinned, but he thought, I hope there won't *be* a next time; not quite like that one, anyway . . .

Setter had steadied, now at three hundred and sixty feet, and MacGregor said, 'Slow ahead together. Two hundred and fifty feet, Number One.'

'Two fifty feet, Sir.'

Hutchin's voice was slightly higher than it had been the last time he spoke. He said, 'They've lost contact, Sir. H.E. on Red five-oh.'

'Starboard ten.' MacGregor crossed to the helmsman, and peered over his shoulder at the compass to see where the ship's head was pointing. ' 'M. Steer one hundred degrees.'

Then he turned back to Hutchins; 'Well, where's the other one now?'

'Must be stopped, Sir . . . Can't hear him, only the one . . . ' Hutchins twisted the dial, his eyes anxious, Adam's apple jerking convulsively.

MacGregor told Wyllie, 'All compartments check and report.'

'Aye aye, Sir.' Wyllie began to talk into the mouthpiece of his telephone set.

Crawshaw reported, 'Depth, Sir, two hundred and fifty feet.'

'Very good.'

Hutchins spoke sharply, 'Enemy Green seven-oh, in contact, stopped . . . other one Red one-six-oh, closing. Both in contact, Sir.'

Crawshaw muttered, 'Here we go again.'

MacGregor growled, '*Blast* them! Half ahead together: port twenty, steer oh-three-oh.'

Wyllie got his report in quickly, 'All compartments correct, Sir. No leaks or damage.'

Soames moved up to stand beside Olsen. He whispered, 'You know, you're a lucky bugger, you are! This is your watch – the rest of us are missing our shut-eye!' He went back to the chart table, humming *Swing Low, Sweet Chariot*.

The trawler went smack over the top of them, this time. MacGregor had turned, in the hope of throwing him off, but the German must have caught on the changing bearing in time to put his own helm over. They heard the screws scrunch overhead, the rhythmic thump-thump-thump of reciprocating engines, as loud as a passing train. Another lot of charges on their way: Olsen jammed himself firmly in the entrance to the gangway, at this end of the chart table. He didn't want to do another of those Cresta Run imitations.

MacGregor said, 'Group up, full ahead together,' and the submarine pulsed as the motors drove her forward through deep, resisting water. The Cox'n, Bird, on his stool at the controls of the after hydroplanes, spoke into the silence of men waiting, 'Captain, Sir?'

MacGregor glanced down at him, surprised. 'Yes, Cox'n?'

'I've a request to make, Sir. I'd like to volunteer for the Fleet Air Arm, Sir.'

Everybody laughed: the tension was such that any attempt at humour was wildly successful. Some of the men were still chuckling when the new pattern of charges exploded.

It wasn't nearly as bad as the first lot had been. The explosions seemed to come from all directions, but in every case from overhead; the enemy, it seemed, were using shallow settings. The firing mechanism on depth-charges was operated by a 'pistol' at the end of the barrel-shaped charge; in essentials it was a container with holes in its outside. When the container was full of water, it fired the charge. To change the depth-setting, you altered the size of the adjustable holes, so that it filled up more slowly when you wanted a deep explosion, or faster for use nearer the surface.

MacGregor grinned cheerfully. 'Starboard twenty. Steer one-four-oh. Group down, slow together.'

Apart from the usual shower of cork chips from the special paint on the deckhead (a mixture designed to absorb condensation which would otherwise form and drip from the flat metal surfaces), the only effect of that last lot of explosions had been to raise everyone's spirits; the near-miss of the first attack had been much too close for comfort or complacency, but now it looked as if that had been no more than a fluke, a lucky shot.

MacGregor said to Crawshaw, 'We'll stick to this depth, for a bit anyway. Bless their little square heads, they think we're at a hundred feet!' Crawshaw nodded. But he thought, It's only a good depth *so far* – until they catch on and set the bloody things deeper.

Setter was steady on her new course and the helmsman reported, 'Course, Sir, one-four-oh.'

'Very good.' MacGregor had a moving picture in his mind: at this moment he could see the first trawler, the one who'd just dropped charges on them, still heading away eastward. The other, which had been stopped and holding the Asdic contact from a position broad on the submarine's starboard bow, would still be down to the south of them, probably waiting jealously to take his turn in the attack. But after the explosions, he'd almost certainly have lost the contact and would have to pick it up again before he could move in. By coming round now to a course of one-four-oh, or south east, MacGregor was aiming *Setter* between the two enemy ships; and with any luck their Asdics might confuse each other, particularly with the sea still disturbed by the criss-crossing of wakes and by the recent depth-charges.

Hutchins's next report confirmed the situation, just as he'd visualised it. 'Transmissions Green four-five, no H.E. The other one's Red five-one, Sir, H.E. fading. Neither of 'em in contact, Sir.'

'Very good.' MacGregor glanced at his watch: five-thirty. Somehow, he had to shake those swine off in time to surface at eight, or soon after that. Well – not necessarily. If it took longer than that, if they were kept down for several hours, then they'd have to make the time up by staying on the surface tomorrow morning. But again – and, *damn it!* – that was wishful thinking. Now that they knew for certain a submarine was here, it was very unlikely they'd give her any peace even if she got away from this bunch reasonably quickly. There'd be aircraft up, swarms of them, and more surface craft out from Trondheim or possibly even closer. MacGregor admitted to himself that the chances of meeting the bishop on time were not by any means bright.

'Where are they now, Hutchins?'

'H.E. Green six-oh, Sir, drawing right . . . Green six-two, now. Transmitting, Sir. Other one: transmitting, no H.E., Red six-one.'

MacGregor snapped his fingers in delight: the one to the South was moving up across *Setter*'s stern – thinking, presumably, that she'd either doubled back on a westerly course or turned to port, northwards. The other trawler hadn't regained contact either, and he was out in the deep field as if he was expecting the submarine to have stayed on her previous course.

The mouse was getting away! MacGregor checked his sudden elation, forced the pleasure out of his eyes. At any moment the Germans might realise their error: failing any contact up there, they'd see that there was only one direction they hadn't thought of and covered. Then, they'd be back.

Hutchins reported again. 'H.E. Green eight-five, Sir, still drawing right. Other one's Red seven-one. Both transmitting.'

Crawshaw turned his head and grinned at the Captain. Seeing it, several men caught the hope and the optimism and exchanged looks of triumph and relief. Soames reached over and tapped Olsen on the shoulder: he whispered, 'Mac's the boy!'

Minutes ticked by, and with the passing of each one MacGregor began to feel more and more hopeful. Each minute meant distance, and a wider area which the enemy would have to search before they could regain contact: in the last five minutes, *Setter* could have turned to any of a dozen widely different courses. The more alternatives there were, the more the room there'd be for confusion in the Germans' thinking.

Hutchins cleared his throat, and said, 'H.E. growing fainter, Sir, Green one hundred. Second H.E., Red nine-five. Both transmitting.'

MacGregor laughed. He hadn't meant to: it had slipped out, and now he was furious that he'd let it; it was still much too early to display confidence . . . All the same, it was the way he felt! The laughter rippled round the Control Room, and to counteract the optimism he'd triggered in the un-guarded moment, MacGregor said gruffly, 'We're not out of the wood, yet.' He jerked his head upwards, towards the surface, and added, 'Those blokes aren't stupid and they haven't bloody well gone home yet.'

Crawshaw asked Bird, 'Still want to go flying, Cox'n?'

'I'll let you know tonight, Sir. When I've had me rum.'

Hutchins said, 'The H.E. on the port side is drawing *right*, Sir, increasing.'

MacGregor swore. That'd teach him to lose hold of him-self! The trawler on the port side was the one that'd dropped the last lot of charges: now, instead of hanging around in the suburbs, he was cutting down this way, either parallel to *Setter*'s course, or converging on it. He asked Hutchins, 'Bearing?'

'Red eight-eight, Sir. H.E.'s gettin' louder. Transmissions, no contact.'

MacGregor mentally supplied the missing word – *yet.*

He asked the Asdic operator, 'The other?'

'Green one-three-five, Sir. Still drawing right. Green one-three-eight . . . one-four-one . . . '

Drawing right, certainly, and much faster than before. That second trawler was going to pass across *Setter*'s stern, by the sound of things; he must have altered course to starboard in the last minutes. It was exactly what Mac-Gregor had hoped would *not* happen, and had begun to think *would* not: they were shifting their sweep to the east and south. Well –

'Starboard fifteen.' Go back up where they've got tired of searching!

'Fifteen of starboard wheel on, Sir.'

'Steer two-nine-oh.' It was a pity; not only had *Setter* been getting away from the hunters, but she'd been getting off in more or less the right direction for her future plans. Now, back into the long grass . . .

MacGregor thought, I'll get out on this course until I've put some distance between us and the trawler that's going South, and then, when the other one will have got out of our way off to the eastward, I'll turn up north and eventually circle back into the right direction . . . It would be nice, of course, and make the whole thing a lot easier, if I could go a bit faster; but he didn't dare, because of the noise which went hand in hand with speed.

The helmsman centred his brass wheel, then put some port wheel on to counteract the swing. Centring it again he reported, 'Course, two-nine-oh, Sir.'

'Very good.'

Hutchins raised his voice. 'Bearings now, Sir, Green one hundred and Green one-six-four. Both drawing right.'

MacGregor nodded. He thought, Ten minutes like this, and then I'll turn up. So far, it's good: not as good as it was, but at least they haven't smelt us. He looked at his watch, to give himself the ten minutes exactly: he was looking at it when Hutchins squawked,

'In contact, Sir, on Green one-oh-five. H.E. slowing . . . '

That top one had found *Setter* and now she was stopping, or slowing down, to hold her like a fish on a line while his pal got back into the game.

'Where's the other?'

'Green one-seven-two, Sir, Transmitting . . . In contact, Sir, they're *both* in contact!'

'Port twenty. Half ahead together.'

You had to admit it: those trawler boys weren't at all bad. Either that or they were bloody lucky! MacGregor decided to repeat the manoeuvre which had worked so well last time: he'd go right round and back to a north-easterly course, aiming between the two of them.

'Steer oh-five-five.'

'Steer oh-five-five, Sir.'

'Slow together.' MacGregor thought, wryly, I was going to spend ten minutes creeping quietly away on a safe course. Now I'm going right under the buggers, and we're going to get another basinful . . .

Hutchins said, 'H.E. right ahead, closing. In contact, H.E. increasing. Sir.'

Here it came. MacGregor glanced round the Control Room; he saw that everyone was holding on to something. He thought of telling Wyllie to warn the men in the other compartments: but there wasn't time, and anyway, they'd hear the enemy ship pass overhead in a minute and they'd know, then, without being told.

The helmsman muttered, 'Course oh-five-five, Sir.' He said it quietly because it was a report he was required to make but he doubted if anyone would attach much importance to it, not just at this moment . . .

When MacGregor heard the enemy's propeller noise, he said, 'Group up. Full ahead together. Starboard twenty.' *Setter* surged ahead and began to swing round fast as the trawler raced across overhead and every man in the submarine thought of those charges rolling out of the stern racks, dropping in the trawler's wake and plumbing down towards them through two hundred and fifty feet of dense, green water.

'Steer one-two-oh.'

'Steer one-two-oh, Sir.' The helmsman let his wheel spin back, centring the rudder; his face stayed calm as he watched the readings and *Setter* eased to the new course.

Hutchins removed the headphones; it was a necessary precaution, before depth-charges went off; he'd lose his eardrums if he forgot it.

MacGregor was watching the circling hand of the stop-watch. He'd started it as the trawler passed over, and he was timing the interval to the bangs –

The first explosion was astern and very close. It flung *Setter*'s tail up, and as the motors were at full ahead and grouped up. she began to dive fast. MacGregor yelled over the noise of more explosions, 'Group down, half ahead together!', and Wyllie, who was sprawled on the deck beside his upturned stool with his left hand trying to hold the telephone set on his head and his right hand clinging to the edge of the for'ard periscope well, struggled into a sitting position and passed the order jerkily to the motor room. Bird, the Cox'n, had the after planes hard over to drag the stern down and level the ship, but so far it wasn't having much or any effect: another charge went off and that was close, too, on the starboard side. It rolled *Setter* over to port and Featherstone was almost lying, more than leaning, on the panel of diving-control instruments on the port side. But it seemed to counteract the effect of the first charge, by pushing the bow up a bit, and now as the submarine steadied and the last charge burst farther away, a loud, ringing clash of sound which shook her and brought down more cork chips like white rain all through the submarine but caused no damage and was nothing in comparison with the first two, she came nearer to an even keel and the needles slowed their frantic rush around the depth-gauges. Four hundred feet, now: fifty below the tested depth, and still going down . . .

Wyllie's telephone spoke in his ear and he muttered into its mouthpiece, 'Right.' MacGregor looked at him enquiringly and Wyllie said, 'After Ends report a slight leak on the port propeller shaft gland, Sir.'

'Ask the engineer officer to go aft.'

'Aye aye, Sir.' Wyllie called the engine room, and gave Chief the Captain's message. Then he got on to the After Ends again and told them, 'Engineer Officer's coming through to you, mate.' They'd have to open the watertight door between those two compartments, to let him through, shut and clip it again behind him.

At a depth of four hundred and thirty feet, Crawshaw had the bow up. He had the ballast pump going, too, to lighten the ship, and after the sudden drastic change in depth it had plenty of work to do. MacGregor snapped 'Full ahead together.' Had to get up fast: for one thing because this depth was unsafe: for another, because that leak would be less dangerous in shallower and therefore less dense water. And there was a further consideration: they'd been at two hundred and fifty feet when those charges went off, and the first one – the one that had done the damage – had exploded *under* the stern. In other words, the

Germans had cottoned-on to *Setter*'s depth.

'One hundred and fifty feet.'

'Hundred and fifty feet, Sir.'

MacGregor saw that she was coming up well, now. If anything too fast. He told Wyllie, 'Slow together.' Crawshaw was busy with the pump telegraph again, flooding the internal tanks to reset the trim for the new depth.

'Where are they, Hutchins?'

'Green one-six-oh, Sir, H.E. fading. Transmitting but not in contact.' That was the one who'd made the attack; she'd run on over and now, with *Setter* steering South-East, she was a long way out on the starboard quarter. 'Second one, Red seven-oh, Sir, stopped and in contact.'

So that one still had them pinned. MacGregor kept the worry out of his face: or tried to. Wyllie told him, 'Engineer Officer would like to speak to you, Sir.'

He took the headphones and held one against his ear, and spoke into the swivelled mouthpiece. 'Yes, Chief?'

'It's better, now, Sir. But it's a nasty leak and I can't vouch for what'll happen if another of those sods goes off anywhere near us. Or if we go deep. When I got here it was fairly spurting in.'

'Can you do anything about it?'

'Nothing useful.'

' 'M . . . Look, Chief –' MacGregor turned his back on the men in the Control Room and dropped his voice to a little more than a whisper. 'Stay there and watch it. I'll try to keep the boat up if I can. But if you think it's getting out of hand, then evacuate the compartment immediately and report to me from the engine room *afterwards*. All right?'

'Aye aye, Sir.'

MacGregor turned and straightened, handed the headset back to Wyllie. Addressing the First Lieutenant, but intending the news for everyone, he said, 'Chief's getting it under control. Nothing to worry about.'

Crawshaw reported, 'Depth one-fifty, Sir.'

Hutchins drew in his breath and said, 'H.E. closing, Sir, Red six-six, in contact. Bearing steady, revs increasing, Sir.' His eyes were wide and there were beads of sweat all over his face.

'One hundred feet. Half ahead together.'

MacGregor didn't usually pray, at times like this. It wasn't that he didn't believe in prayer – far from it – but more that he was where he was, and in the capacity of Commanding Officer, simply because he was considered capable of taking the submarine to do its job and bringing it and its crew back again all in one piece. He did his praying in quiet moments, and at times like this (not that he remembered having had a moment *quite* like this, before) he resisted the urge to ask for help because every one of his actions and thoughts was needed by and devoted to the job in hand, which, at this moment, was to save the ship and the lives of the men in her. He'd said his prayers, last night and every night and quite frequently at other times as well: he'd put things in general terms in God's hands, and now it was up to him to attend to the details as they came along.

The prayer which he would have liked to have offered now was simply, Please, let this next lot of charges be set *deep*: let them think we're still down at two hundred and fifty feet.

Instead, he heard the enemy's screws coming closer, louder: he saw the eyes all round him drifting upwards towards the deckhead as if they thought to *see* the swine as he passed over: he waited until the propeller noise had reached a crescendo and he ordered, 'Group up, full ahead together! Port twenty!'

Immediately he wondered if he'd made a mistake in ordering the burst of speed. With the gland on the port propeller shaft leaking, high revolutions wouldn't improve its chances of holding out . . .

But, hell! Can't go deep – can't go fast – what the devil *can* I do?

The answer, of course, was quite simple. Unwilling as he was to admit it even to himself, there was no disguising the fact that *Setter* was in serious trouble and that it was going to get a lot worse before it could possibly get any better. One bit of damage that reduced the submarine's manoeuvrability made her an easier target for the enemy: an easier target for them meant that there'd be more damage soon, unless some extraordinary fluke of luck stepped in to help her: it was a vicious circle and exactly what the enemy was aiming for.

He wiped the sweat out of his eyes, then grasped the ladder with both hands and stiffened his mind against the explosions; he saw that all their eyes were on him and he grinned at Olsen, but he was thinking and hating the truth of the thought, *There's bloody little I can do to get us out of this –*

12

KORVETTENKAPITÄN von Strehssen looked old for his rank; as, indeed, he was. If it had not been for the machinations of that lunatic, the Führer, he would have been enjoying by now an easy and peaceful retirement, which was the one thing to which he had looked forward all through his naval career. He hadn't joined the Navy to become an Admiral or to win medals: the whole project had been his father's, or perhaps his grandfather's, at a time when he himself was still in the cradle and consequently was not consulted or told anything about it. But by the time he was four he'd known all about all of it, and from that stage it seemed to him now whenever he looked back on it, which he did more and more frequently, that he had sprung almost directly from a pram into a suit of uniform; and now here he was, well past retiring age, Naval Officer in Charge of this miserable little Norwegian port and a couple of desolate islands, with nobody to talk to and a complete absence of any of those small pleasures in life, simple ones, to which he felt entitled. He'd been swindled, made victim from birth to a confidence trick which still had him in its clutches: he had looked to retirement not as an end to his active life, but as the beginning of a life which he would be able to call his own . . .

At this moment, however, the Korvettenkapitän's habitual expression of impatient misery had been replaced by one of pleasurable excitement. Looking up from the signal which his young assistant had placed before him on the otherwise bare desk, he saw in the young man's face a reflection of his own delight.

'This is splendid! Magnificent!'

'It certainly is, Sir. Indeed so. If I may, Sir, I'll go back in case there's more news.'

'By all means, my dear fellow. I'll be along myself, in a minute. First I'd better telephone –' he stopped his sentence in mid-air, but added mentally, 'That swine Grauermann.' He said, to finish the sentence, 'Oslo.'

The young man's smile faded. 'Do you think that wise,

Sir?' He looked worried, like a baby missing its bottle. 'In view of what –'

Von Strehssen waved an elegant hand in the air. 'Of course . . . You go on, boy.'

'Sir.' The youngster clicked his heels. '*Heil Hitler!*'

'Eh?' The Korvettenkapitän had picked up the telephone. 'Oh, yes. Yes, of course. I mean, *Heil Hitler*. As the door closed, there was a click from the instrument in his hand, and the operator came on the line. Von Strehssen told him, 'Get Oslo on this thing, please. I wish to speak to Kapitän zur See Grauermann.' He dropped the instrument back into its cradle and thought, For once, I *do* want to speak to him! What I've got to tell him will make his childish hush-hush plans look like the hot air they really are!

Von Strehssen felt for Kapitän zur See Grauermann a warm, personal loathing such as he had seldom felt for anyone, even in a long career of frustrations and irritations. It wasn't just that Grauermann was his superior officer as well as ten years younger than he was, but also that the Kapitän zur See was a go-getter, a climber, a Party man, and more often than not extremely offensive. What was more, he looked like a frog.

.   .   .   .

'Herr Kapitän zur See Grauermann?'

'*Ja?*'

'Von Strehssen, here.'

'So.' The tone was flat. 'And what do *you* want? You've had my orders, haven't you? Eh?'

'Yes, Sir. But –'

'*But?*'

Von Strehssen gritted his teeth for a moment. Then he

114

said, 'The aircraft have been grounded, Sir, in accordance with your instructions. However, just as we were about to transmit the signal to the A/S Group, we received a signal *from them.*'

It sounded as if Grauermann had just spat, and then yawned. It was quite possible that he had. 'Well, what's that got to do with it? Can't you handle your own piddling little affairs, man?'

'The signal reports that they have detected an enemy submarine and are attacking it with depth-charges. *At this moment*, Sir!'

There was a silence from the other end of the line. After a moment, von Strehssen asked, 'Are you there, Sir? I said they are *in contact, now!*' He was smiling as he spoke. So Grauermann had been taken aback, as he'd expected: for once, the swine was at a loss for anything to say!

'Yes, von Strehssen, I am here . . . Answer me a question, will you?'

'Gladly, Sir.'

'What are orders for?'

The Korvettenkapitän thought, I've often wondered. But he said, quickly, 'To be obeyed, Sir.'

'To be obeyed . . . Yes, indeed. And, tell me: have *you* obeyed *my* orders?'

'I – well, Sir under the –'

'*Have you?*'

'Under these circumstances – *no.*'

'And are you aware of the penalty for disobedience of orders in time of war, Korvettenkapitän von Strehssen?'

'Sir: the submarine has been detected. You were not aware of that when you gave the order in question. Consequently, and since it is my duty to endeavour to achieve the destruction of the enemy, I have now telephoned to inform you of the new situation which prevails.'

There was another silence, which, this time, von Strehssen did not break. When Grauermann spoke, it was in a quiet, deliberately controlled tone which was far more menacing than his usual shouts and bellows.

'Von Strehssen . . . Out of every five hundred attacks with depth-charges, perhaps one is successful. The odds against this present attack succeeding are therefore in the region of five hundred to one. On the other hand, it will certainly warn the submarine that we are expecting it, and if its Commanding Officer is not a raving lunatic it will presumably remove itself with great alacrity as soon as those depth-charges of yours are all used up: it will escape, instead of coming into the trap which I have prepared for it with the full co-operation and support of our Admiral. A trap, von Strehssen, from which it *could not escape*. So, you see what you have probably done? What you have, in fact, *endeavoured to achieve*?'

'Sir – I –'

'Be quiet! Now – carry out my orders, *immediately*. It is just possible that you may not have succeeded in wrecking the entire operation. If the submarine is *not* sunk by U-331: and she is halfway there, by now, on her way from Trondheim at eighteen knots: if that English submarine escapes, von Strehssen, I'll have you court-martialled the day after tomorrow, here in Oslo . . . Meanwhile – *call off those damned trawlers!*'

The line clicked, and went dead.

13

'Steer north.'

The helmsman let the wheel slip round through his

fingers to take the twenty degrees of port rudder off, and he opened his mouth to acknowledge the order: before he could speak, the charges exploded.

They were loud enough, and if the earlier attacks had not been so much closer they might have been alarming; but the trawler hadn't made a good shot, this time. One charge went off astern of *Setter*, and the rest of them on her starboard quarter: if she hadn't been turned by that time on to the new course they'd have been on her starboard side, the whole pattern of them, which meant that the enemy had overshot the submarine's track to start with and that the turn and the increased speed had thrown them even farther out.

They were deep explosions, too, so obviously the enemy hadn't been quick enough to recognise *Setter*'s change of depth.

'Group down. Slow together.'

Wyllie passed the order to the motor room, and when he'd done it MacGregor told him, 'Call the After Ends and ask the Engineer Officer to speak to me.' Although those charges had been a good distance off, MacGregor was worried that the first one, astern, might have given that end enough of a jolt to make the leak worse. Chief came to the line, and he asked him, 'How is it, now?'

'About the same, Sir. That lot didn't do us any harm.'

'Good. All right, Chief.' He gave the 'phones back to Wyllie, and looked over at Hutchins, raising his eyebrows to ask the obvious question.

'Red one-five-oh, Sir, H.E. decreasing. Stopping, I think. Not in contact.' That was the one who'd just attacked. 'Red one hundred, Sir, H.E. closing, revs increasing. In contact.'

' 'M ...' It was coming at them from the port beam, this

time – if *Setter* stayed on the same course. The number two trawler had been lying stopped, since its last run over; it had held the contact and now without giving them any more of a rest than it could help it was coming in again.

They seem to do it the same way each time, MacGregor thought: it must be a system they've worked out between them, and which they never vary. When each one has made his attack, he runs on out on his attacking course, then stops and picks up the contact again and holds it, stopped, while his pal has a bash. Turn and turn about, and after *you*, Claud!

A light of hope came into MacGregor's eyes as the idea took hold of him . . .

Surface ships *shouldn't* stop, when submarines are about. They ought to know better! Probably they thought it was safe enough, while the other member of the team was keeping the submarine deep and busy; but they were wrong, there, very wrong indeed, and if *Setter* could take advantage now of this glaring error in their tactics, she might, after all, get away with a whole skin. And, at the same time, give Jerry something to think about.

There was plenty of risk in it. But the way things were, it was a matter of appreciating that a risk with a chance of success was a great deal better than continuing to play Aunt Sally until a charge came close enough to finish the game.

'Sixty feet, Number One.'

'Sixty feet – Sir!' Crawshaw's voice rose with the surprise in it.

'Starboard ten.'

Starboard ten, Sir . . . Ten of starboard wheel on, Sir.'

'Stand by numbers one and two tubes.'

The men glanced at each other in surprise; and Crawshaw turned to the Captain with a look of enquiry in his face. But MacGregor ignored it, and Wyllie passed the order for'ard excitedly, as if he liked the idea although he hadn't an inkling of what lay behind it.

'Where're they now, Hutchins?' MacGregor told the helmsman, 'Steer oh-eight-oh.'

'Steer oh-eight-oh, Sir.'

Olsen grinned, suddenly. He'd caught on, or he thought he had; and it delighted him. Being new to submarines and brand new to depth-charging, he was quite unaccustomed to this passive, suffering role: to twisting and turning and taking punishment like a dog on a rope and not being able to hit back. His emotions in the last hour or so had been compounded more of anger than of fear, though the latter element had been a fairly powerful ingredient too.

Hutchins said, 'Red nine-five, Sir, H.E. growing louder.'

'Other one still stopped?'

'Yes, Sir.' MacGregor nodded, pleased. He told the helmsman, 'Steer oh-eight-five,' to put *Setter*'s stern straight at the approaching enemy. He thought, They're doing the same again. With any luck, they'll repeat it now. That bugger'll run over and drop his bloody charges and when he stops I'll have a crack at him before the other one comes in again. It's unlikely I'll hit him, firing blind, but there's a chance; and even if I miss he'll realise that we're capable of firing on an Asdic bearing and from deep; it'll shake him up and possibly make them change their tactics. Whatever they change to, it can only be an improvement on this.

Crawshaw reported, 'Sixty feet, Sir!', and Wyllie said, 'Numbers one and two tubes ready, Sir.'

'Very good.'

By heading directly away from the direction of the

attack, on the same course as the enemy's, *Setter* would be pointing in more or less the right direction for the shot. But, MacGregor thought, I'll try and throw him off a bit, first ... When he heard the trawler's screws, he told the helmsman, 'Port ten.'

'Port ten, Sir.'

With any luck the enemy would detect this swing off-course and put his own wheel over too: MacGregor let the propeller noise get really loud and then he snapped, 'Hard a-starboard!'

'Hard a-starboard, Sir!' The helmsman dragged the brass wheel over to reverse the direction of the turn.

'Group up, full ahead together!'

The trawler had passed over, and by now the depth-charges would be on their way down. If the enemy had got a true idea of *Setter*'s depth, a mere sixty feet, it wouldn't be long before those things went off ...

It wasn't. The sea itself seemed to explode all round the submarine: the charges burst with hardly any interval between each explosion and all that was obvious was that they were very close indeed. *Setter* shook like a jelly and rang like a gong: the hull trembled and the deckboards seemed to shift under their feet. She was diving, going down like a rocket in reverse, her bow hard down and the needles flying round the gauges. Men were sprawled all over the Control Room, cursing quietly, struggling for handholds and for footing on the tilting, trembling deck. The gyro alarm went off, a hideous, ear-splitting shriek of the electric bell which was a warning that the great fly-wheel of the main compass had been thrown out of action: Soames sprang to the cage which housed the gyro controls, and broke the switch to stop the noise: the helmsman went on steering by the magnetic card instead.

MacGregor shouted, 'Group down! Slow together!' With this much angle on the boat, the screws were only driving her deeper. The gauges read two hundred feet: the fore 'planesman, Hallet, was off his stool, bent over the control wheel, fighting against it: he gasped, 'Fore 'planes jammed hard a-dive, Sir!' Crawshaw jumped forward and added his strength to Hallet's, but the wheel was jammed solid: two hundred and sixty feet on the gauges and they couldn't shift it: *Setter* was ploughing deeper every second.

MacGregor told Wyllie, 'Stop together. Group up. Full astern together.' He looked at the depth-gauge: two-ninety, two-ninety-five, three hundred: the submarine was going down as fast as a lift in a skyscraper.

The motors went astern, racing, and the dive slowed: MacGregor turned to Wyllie again and said, 'Fore 'planes in hand.' Wyllie called the Fore Ends and gave them the order, and Hallet gave up the pointless struggle with the control wheel. They were going to rig the emergency control system: he plugged in the emergency telephone set and clipped the 'phones over his ears, so that he could talk to them and tell them which way to angle the 'planes when they were ready to start. *Setter* was hanging, now, bow-down at a steep angle, still sinking slowly but with the screw churning astern to drag her back. Mac-Gregor his face running with sweat, said, 'Group down. Full astern together.' He was tempted to put some air into number one Main Ballast, but he'd try everything else first. Meanwhile, he didn't want to tear the guts out of the battery.

Hallet muttered into his telephone, 'O.K. . . . Go on trying till y'bloody well *do*, mate.' He looked up and told MacGregor 'They say they can't budge 'em, Sir.'

Olsen stepped forward. 'Shall I go there, Sir?'

'Yes, Olsen. Quick as you can.'

The Norwegian hurried past the wardroom to the bulk-head door which led for'ard to the accommodation space: he unscrewed the valve on the tiny voicepipe which pierced the bulkhead itself and which was intended, chiefly, to be used to detect the presence of water in case the next compartment might be flooded: you opened it, and if a jet of water shot out of it you knew better than to open the door: he whistled through it, then shouted to the men on the other side, 'Open up!' While he dragged the heavy clips off this side of the door he heard them doing the same on their side: he heaved, and the door swung open. They shut it and clipped it again behind him as he went on for'ard down the steeply angled gangway, past the Ladies' Boudoir and the other messes. The next door led into the Fore Ends and again he opened the tube and whistled for the inside clips to be removed.

Behind him, someone asked, 'What's up, Sir? We all right?' The last clip came off and as the door opened Olsen said, 'Sure, we're all right.' The door swung shut again behind him and he put the clips on himself because the man who'd opened it for him on this side had already gone back to join the others who were straining at the heavy steel bars on the hydroplanes' emergency control.

Where the 'planes hinged into the hull, the boss of each pivot projected into the compartment. There was one on each side, port and starboard, and in each boss was a slot designed to take the end of a bar which could be fitted there to act as a lever for swinging the planes to and fro by muscle-power. Normally it took only one man on each side of the bars to handle it; now they had two on the port side and three on the other: they were heaving and strain-ing, slipping on the tilted deck: sweat ran down their faces and the shirts stuck to their backs, veins bulged in their necks and foreheads: but the planes weren't moving.

'Have you opened the by-pass?'

Hughes nodded. 'Yes, Sir. Bloody things are stuck solid, though. Reckon they're bent . . . '

Olsen tried the by-pass valve that had to be open to free the 'planes from telemotor pressure before they could be moved by hand; he found it was still threequarters shut. The small brass wheel was hellishly stiff and for that reason they'd thought it was fully open when it wasn't. Olsen put a wheelspanner on it and wrenched it round.

'Be O.K., now. Together – one, two, six – *heave!*'

The bars swung down easily enough now, and Olsen told the torpedoman who had the telephone set on his head, 'Tell the Control Room fore 'planes ready in hand, hard a-rise.'

The watertight doors to the tube space were shut: Olsen got one of them open and went through to see Rawlinson. The T.I. was perched up on his seat between the tubes: the last order from the Control Room had been to stand by numbers one and two, and that was what he was doing, although *Setter* had done some peculiar things since the order came, and was now standing on her snout, pointing at the sea bed and obviously in trouble. But the T.I. was right: he'd had an order and it hadn't been cancelled.

He asked Olsen, calmly, 'We looping the loop, Sir?'

The Norwegian laughed. 'Almost. Fore 'planes jammed up. In hand, now.'

'Ah.' The T.I. nodded, slowly. 'Much other damage, Sir?'

'No . . . we're all right, T.I.'

'What's the stand-by tubes for, Sir – d'you know?'

'I think the Captain is going to have a shot at one of the trawlers. I think he will do it, now.'

'Ah.' The T.I. had an accurate appreciation of things, now. The fore 'planes were jammed, and there was other damage too: this lad had lied when he'd said 'No.' He wasn't a good liar, and it had shown in his face. Consequently, the other damage must be serious, or he wouldn't have bothered to deny it. Finally, Mac was thinking of firing torpedoes at one of the hunting craft, and that was an indication that he was in a fairly desperate state of mind.

'I must go back, now.' The T.I. nodded at him, and grinned, and Olsen stepped through into the Fore Ends and clipped the door shut again. He noticed that the 'planes were being handled easily, now, by only one man on each side. The others were sitting on the deck, waiting to take their turns at the job.

Hughes was cleaning his nails with a clasp-knife. He looked up and asked Olsen casually, 'We're gettin' slightly —ed up, Sir, ain't we?'

Olsen shook his head. 'Not now. It was just some lucky shots they had, that's all.' He told Hughes, 'You owe a six-pence, I think.'

As he went back aft the angle lessened all the time, and when he reached the Control Room *Setter* was on an even keel at four hundred and ten feet. Well below her safe diving depth, but she was under control now, and Mac-Gregor was saying, 'Half ahead together. Two hundred feet.'

Hallet muttered into his phone, 'Ease to fifteen degrees o'rise.' He passed orders to the man for'ard, telling him to move the 'planes exactly as he'd be moving them himself if the main controls were still working. There was a slight time lag, but apart from that it worked well enough.

The needles were beginning to swing the other way. MacGregor looked round the Control Room, grimly taking stock. Featherstone had twisted his foot, perhaps sprained the ankle: he stood on one leg, scowling: Crawshaw had a deep gash across his forehead and he was holding a balled handkerchief there to keep the blood out of his eyes. (He'd been pumping so hard on the for'ard tank that there wasn't much left in it, and now as *Setter* rose he was gradually putting the weight back.) These were the visible signs, and the things of least importance; there'd be similar small casualties, in the other compartments, and a lot of things smashed. But the main damage – jammed fore 'planes: gyro out of action: stern gland leaking.

MacGregor took the 'phone from Wyllie and spoke to Chief again as the boat rose past three hundred feet. Chief told him, 'A minute ago I was going to evacuate. It was bloody awful, and getting worse. Now it's slowed to a trickle. We'll hang on.'

MacGregor asked Hutchins, 'Where are they?' The Asdic operator looked puzzled as he twiddled the dial of his set. He shook his head, and told the Captain, 'Can't hear nothing, Sir.' He turned the control again, and started, his eyes opening wide as he said, '*Yes*, Sir . . . Green one-oh-five, H.E., but it's faint, Sir, a long way off.'

'The other one's probably nearer. Come on, find him!' MacGregor thought, The bugger's sitting right on top of us, I expect. Can't be far away . . .

The Cox'n twisted his head sideways and muttered to Crawshaw, 'That was three or four rum jars broke, Sir, by the sound of it. 'Orrible crash, it was, and no mistaking it . . . Reckon we can 'ave what's left in 'em tonight, Sir, when we surface?'

Everyone laughed, and Crawshaw glanced round at the

Captain with his eyebrows raised. MacGregor stepped up beside the Cox'n and clapped a hand on the man's shoulder.

'Cox'n, that's a bloody good idea. We'll scoff the lot . . . Well, splice the mainbrace, anyway.'

He thought, I'll see Bird gets a D.S.M., for that suggestion . . . if not something better. If he can think like that – talk like that – what the hell am I getting so bloody worried about?

In that moment he decided that he was going to have another crack at sinking one of those trawlers.

.   .   .   .

'Steer east.'

'Steer east, Sir.'

MacGregor looked at Hutchins. 'D'you think the set's all right?'

Hutchins nodded violently. The Captain went over to him and slid the spare set of 'phones over his own ears: they were alive, all right. He told the operator, 'Train all round, slowly.'

Hutchins stopped at the bearing of Green four-two. He muttered, 'There it is, Sir. Very faint now, goin' away. Can't 'ardly 'ear it, can you?'

The sound of the screws was so faint that there couldn't be any doubt about it: at least one of the trawlers was going away, to the south east. It could be both of them: at that distance the sound of the two ships would be merged into one.

They couldn't have lost contact and be searching over there: first because they couldn't have lost it, when they'd been on to *Setter* so closely and when she'd been unmanoeuvrable, incapable of dodging, an almost static target and making a hell of a noise too, one way and another; and secondly because if they *had* been so clumsy as to have lost the contact they'd hardly be looking for her now a couple of miles or more away.

'Go on sweeping all round.' He thought again, That could be only one of them, and the other sitting up there waiting for us . . . but if they *are* going home, it must be either that they think they've sunk us, or that they've used up all their depth-charges. They were pretty small ships, and it was possible they didn't carry many.

There was no sound from any other direction. Mac-Gregor put down the 'phones.

'One hundred feet.'

'Hundred feet, Sir.'

The needles crept around the gauges as the submarine rose slowly, quietly, towards the surface. Soames appeared out of the machinery space below the after end of the Control Room: he told the Captain, cheerfully, 'Gyro's O.K. now, Sir.'

'Sure?' MacGregor sounded surprised.

'It only had a bit of a wobble, I think, Sir. Probably straightened itself out again almost at once. It's right as rain, now.'

It was hard to believe. Ten minutes ago, they'd been in real trouble: flooding aft, gyro out of action, fore 'planes jammed and the boat diving out of control: not to mention the fact that the battery must be just about flat. Mac-Gregor'd been thinking of last resorts: each of the enemy's attacks had seemed closer than the last, and it would have needed only one more close pattern, some further damage and loss of control or the after ends properly flooded, to have put the lid on it for all of them. Now, unbelievably, they'd been reprieved . . .

'Sixty feet.'

'Sixty feet, Sir.'

'Slow together.'

'Slow ahead together, Sir.'

He went to the Asdics again and put on the spare head-set. It wasn't that he didn't trust Hutchins; it was just that the enemy's sudden departure was so astonishing that he found it almost impossible to accept as a fact. But he listened carefully, a complete circuit of the compass, and heard nothing. Even those distant propeller noises to the south east were inaudible, now.

Crawshaw reported, 'Sixty feet, Sir.'

'Very good.' MacGregor checked the time on his watch: seven forty. He thought, If one trawler has stayed behind, lying stopped up there – well, I'll give him a chance to get impatient. Ten minutes on a straight course, at slow speed, a sitting duck to tempt him into motion.

The ten minutes dragged by in heavy silence: he leant on the ladder, in that characteristic position of his with one foot resting on the bottom rung and his right arm way up over his head, like an ape hanging in a tree. The men relaxed, watching him, hoping for the best and waiting for the next move. When for the seventh time MacGregor looked at his watch, ten minutes had gone by. He extricated himself from the ladder, and drew a deep breath.

'Thirty two feet, Number One.'

'Thirty two feet, Sir.'

MacGregor told him, 'I'd take it gently, if I were you . . . Remember the 'planes are in hand.'

'Aye aye, Sir.'

The needles swung slowly anti-clockwise and as they passed the forty-foot mark the Captain moved over to the after periscope. He glanced at Featherstone, and raised his hands, and the glistening, oily tube came hissing up.

Crawshaw called the depths to him. 'Thirty-six feet: thirty-five: thirty-four: thirty-three and a half . . .' The men watching saw sunlight reflected brightly in the Captain's eyes as the top lens broke surface. Olsen, at that moment and for the first time that he'd recorded it in his conscious mind, realised that he hadn't been certain, a little while ago, of ever seeing that light again.

'Thirty-two feet, Sir!'

MacGregor swept all round, fast: then again, rather more slowly. There was nothing there, except sea and sky patched with grey cloud. He pushed up the handles and went to the other periscope, the big one. This time he swept with minute care, searching every foot of the sea and horizon.

'Bring her up to twenty-eight feet, Number One.'

'Twenty-eight feet, Sir.'

With the few extra feet, a much wider horizon . . . But still, an empty sea.

MacGregor stepped back. 'Down periscope.' He rubbed a hand over his eyes, and told them, 'It's a peach of an evening. And we've got the place to ourselves . . .'

They were all grinning at each other. The Captain said, 'Thirty feet. Open up from depth-charging. Watch Diving. We'll surface in half an hour.'

14

'STAND by to surface!'

They were at Diving Stations again: apart from the for'ard hydroplanes being in emergency control, and

Crawshaw having a long strip of sticking-plaster on his forehead, there were no signs of the recent disturbances. The only thing that made the scene in the Control Room slightly odd, out of routine, was that several more men had shaved in the last half hour, and now such a high proportion of the crew had smooth, clean chins that the ones who had not yet come to terms with razors and hot water were as conspicuous as tramps in a first class railway carriage.

Olsen leant with his shoulder against the glass face of the Fruit Machine, watching and listening as the reports came in, preparatory to the act of surfacing: vents shut, blows open . . . Olsen felt a pleasurable excitement, partly in a sense of relief or escape, and partly from the fact that as soon as tomorrow morning they'd be meeting their passengers. He fingered the line of his jaw, which was still whiskered, and told himself that her name wouldn't be Ingrid and that she'd either be seven years old or as ugly as sin. He grinned to himself, thinking, Well – perhaps only a *little* bit ugly . . .

Crawshaw had been ticking off points in his mind as the reports reached him. Now the picture was complete and he told the Captain, 'Ready to surface, Sir.' MacGregor, hunched at the big periscope, grunted an acknowledgement. He was making absolutely sure that there was nothing on the sea or in the sky, because the minutes of surfacing put the submarine in her most vulnerable state. From the time he put the periscope down until he was up there with the glasses at his eyes in the wet and dripping bridge, she'd have no eyes at all.

The reason Olsen hadn't shaved yet was that he'd kept the watch in the Control Room since they'd opened up from depth-charging. He'd missed his own watch, the First Dog, completely, and so he'd relieved Crawshaw who'd been hard at it for several hours, battling with the trim all through the attack; also, Crawshaw had needed to get something done to the gash on his head. That had been the Cox'n's job, swabbing it with iodine then applying lint and plaster. Cox'ns did a short course of doctoring: dressings and drugs, and simple treatments, and they were equipped, too, with a sort of Do-it-Yourself surgeon's kit of knives and scalpels and a textbook which told them how to remove everything from appendices to bullets . . . Crawshaw had sworn, when the iodine was poured into the open wound, and as soon as it was done and plastered the Cox'n had taken a bob off him, for the swear-box.

Now Crawshaw was back in his place to surface the boat, and Soames, who was going to have the first hour of the watch on the surface, was struggling into an Ursula suit, in the wardroom. Soames had missed half of his own watch, too, while the attack was on, so he'd be on the bridge until Crawshaw had eaten some supper.

'Down periscope. Surface!'

The signalman shoved the lower hatch open and stepped aside so that MacGregor could get up the ladder first. Crawshaw told Featherstone, 'Blow one, three and five!'

The E.R.A. opened the high-pressure blows to the main ballast tanks and the air rushed noisily through the pipes and into the tops of the tanks. The hydroplanes were hard a-rise and MacGregor was out of sight, up in the conning tower on the ladder, right under the upper hatch: he'd already got one of its clips off and had his fingers on the pin that secured the other. Below him on the ladder was the signalman, his boots level with the lower hatch.

Crawshaw stood right under it, close to the foot of the ladder, and as *Setter* approached the surface he called the depths up so that MacGregor'd know when to open the top hatch. Most of the men in the Control Room had cigarettes ready, unlit, in their mouths: when the hatch was open, they'd light up, and, as usual, it'd be the best cigarette they'd ever smoked ...

'Stop blowing one and five!'

Featherstone wrenched the valves shut. The top hatch clanged back as MacGregor took off the second clip and let the pressure in the submarine do the rest: for a second, as that pressure rushed out, he'd be holding tightly to the ladder in order not to be blown out himself like the cork out of a bottle of champagne. Water splashed down into the Control Room, it ran down the sides of the ladder and dripped off the rungs: the signalman's boots vanished upwards as he followed the Captain into the bridge: at the same moment the diesels roared into noisy life and cold, fresh air came rushing down through the open hatch.

'Stop blowing three! Open all L.P. master blows!'

Setter rocked gently on the surface, still not right up but already surging ahead under the power of the diesels. Here in the Control Room a dozen matches flared, hands cupped to shield them from the violent draught. Sellers, the messenger, held a bucket under the lower end of the voicepipe, by the helmsman's ear: he opened the stopcock and the water that rushed out was exactly enough to fill the bucket. Careless helmsmen had been known to open that cock without remembering about the water that was trapped in the top of it; but after the cold, salt and unexpected bath which resulted they never forgot about it twice.

The Captain's voice floated out of the dripping copper tube.

'Four hundred and twenty revolutions! Officer of the watch on the bridge!'

Soames had been waiting for that; he jumped on to the

ladder and vanished upwards through the hatch. The Captain yelled again, 'Control Room!'

'Control Room?'

'Send up the lookouts . . . Patrol Routine.'

.   .   .   .

Chief was muttering angrily to himself when he arrived in the wardroom. He flopped down on the end of the bench and grumbled, 'Four hundred and twenty revs – what's he trying to do, shake us to bits?'

Supper was due in at any moment, judging by the smell and the clatter of dishes in the galley. Olsen and Crawshaw were sitting at the table waiting for it, and MacGregor was still on the bridge with Soames.

Crawshaw glanced at the engineer, raising his eyebrows. 'Why, Chief? Aren't your engines up to it?'

Chief snorted. 'Perhaps you didn't know, but the port stern gland is on the blink. So now we go hell for leather and try to shake the bloody thing right out. Who has to sit on it while we're being depth-charged, for God's sake?' Nobody answered, so he asked another question in the same angry tone. 'Where's supper? Eh? . . . *Ellis – supper!*'

The messman didn't hear: those diesels were making far too much noise. Chief closed his eyes, and they were still shut when MacGregor clumped in, pulling off the wet jacket of his Ursula suit. He slapped the engineer on the back, and Chief's eyes snapped open as he grabbed the edge of the table for support. 'What the – ! Oh . . . Look, Sir, this speed –'

'I know, Chief. I know.' MacGregor dropped into the only chair, a thing made of tubular steel, and rubbed the salt out of his eyes. 'Only for an hour or so. I want to get the hell away from where we were. Then we'll come down to three-six-oh revs and slap on a charge.' He looked at the First Lieutenant. 'How's the box?' He meant the battery.

'Not as low as it might be, Sir, considering that long group-up astern.'

'Glad to hear it. You'll have a running charge for six hours, maybe seven . . . Look, Chief. You're privileged – you don't have to shave, since for some reason you choose to resemble an old broom. But you've bloody well got to *wash* that beaver of yours. It's dripping with oil fuel . . . '

The Cox'n came aft from his mess and stopped behind the Captain's chair. He coughed.

'Captain, Sir? Up spirits?'

MacGregor twisted round, and looked up at him. 'Oh. Yes, Cox'n, of course. Have you – er – checked the breakages?'

Bird's smile was only in his eyes. 'Yes, Sir. One jar only, smashed up a bit. Could 'a sworn there'd be more . . . But one, Sir.'

'Write it off, Cox'n. I suppose there's *some* left in it?'

'Just a drop, Sir.'

'Yes. There usually is, isn't there? Well – splice the mainbrace.'

'Aye aye, Sir.' He paused. 'Can I put it over the Tannoy, Sir?'

'Yes.' A moment later they heard the click of the loudspeaker as the Cox'n switched it on in the Control Room: the speakers hummed and throbbed with the noise of the diesels, then the Cox'n's voice roared through the submarine's compartments.

'Up spirits! Splice the bleedin' mainbrace!' At once a hoarse chorus of cheers floated back from the for'ard messes; it was answered by shouts of pleasure from the Control Room. MacGregor edged his chair forward, to be clear of the gangway when the rush came.

It meant that a jar of rum would be officially recorded as having been smashed during the depth-charging. Since it was shattered, the rum no longer existed. Therefore, the mainbrace could be spliced: in other words, there'd be a double tot, neat, for every man. That included officers, who were not normally entitled to rum at all, and in any case never drank at sea.

MacGregor looked at Olsen, who was smiling. The Captain shook his head. 'Sorry, Olsen. Officers excluded. We'll have ours when we get back to Lerwick . . . Anyone got a fag?'

Crawshaw flipped a packet across the table, and they all lit up. Crawshaw said, 'That was a bit close, this afternoon. Eh?'

MacGregor blew a cloud of smoke at the overhead lamp, and watched it hazing around the bulb. 'Close-ish, Number One. Wouldn't want it any closer . . . Those bastards were smarter than most, blast 'em!'

'I can't work out why they sugared off like that. Just when they had us groggy. D'you think they thought they'd sunk us?'

'Could be . . . ' MacGregor asked Chief, 'Would you say it was possible we lost any oil?'

'Uh-uh.' The engineer's brownish beard wagged like a dog's tail. 'Certainly not enough to give 'em *that* idea.'

'Well, then –' Crawshaw suggested, 'they might've run out of charges.'

' 'M.' MacGregor nodded, without much conviction. 'I dare say that's nearer the mark.'

He thought, Near, more likely than the other one; but still not the answer. The sum of charges dropped didn't add up to what two trawlers would carry. Not to half of it!

There was of course the possibility that they'd not had their normal load on board – but that, too, was unlikely. After all, they'd been sweeping for submarines, or for *a submarine*, actively searching. It hadn't been an accidental encounter. So presumably they'd have been equipped for the job: and they couldn't have started with a full load and used some of them in an earlier encounter, because there wasn't any other submarine north of the Shetlands. They hadn't been exercising, either, because if they had been, and dropped charges, the explosions would have been heard from miles away on *Setter*'s asdics.

Together with the activity of those seaplanes earlier in the day, it added up to a riddle which lacked any sort of solution. It was an extraordinary situation, and in the simple puzzles of submarine tactics such conundrums couldn't exist: you knew what you were after, and you knew how the enemy could stop you doing it, or try to, and for any change in the enemy's counter-activity there'd normally be at least one obvious and several reasonable explanations. This time, there wasn't any at all.

MacGregor had two responsibilities in the immediate situation. First – his orders, which were to meet the fishing boat and embark those Norwegians. Second – or possibly this one came first – he had the overriding responsibility for the safety of the ship and her crew. He wouldn't be expected to carry out orders if, being on the spot and in touch with circumstances unknown to the man who'd issued the orders, he was convinced that carrying them out or trying to do that would mean throwing away the submarine and the forty-two men in her. That wouldn't benefit the Almighty Himself, let alone one of His bishops.

Yet to retire from an operation of this sort, you needed a pretty solid reason. On the face of it, there wasn't one. Well, there'd been some air activity – and it had stopped. Then a couple of A/S trawlers, sweeping for submarines, had done their best to sink *Setter*, very nearly succeeded, and broken off the attack for no apparent reason. Behind both those things, the fact that the enemy should not be expecting submarines in these waters, anyway, at this time of year.

It didn't add up to a reason for disobeying orders.

And yet, MacGregor knew: it was certainty, a matter beyond doubt or conjecture, but unsupported by anything which would support him in the black and white of the Patrol Report: he *knew* that he was taking his ship into trouble. It struck him as odd that he should be so sure of it; he had no claim to psychic power or to any degree of intuition. He was not particularly sensitive, nor easily worried . . . So perhaps there *was* a reason, something unrecognised but registered in his subconscious – something beyond a sailor's sniffing at the wind? A logical reason for a growing fear –

There, it was out: at least in his mind, and to himself, he'd used the word!

Perhaps if he talked about it, made the others turn it over in their minds, this thing might come out in a form which he could identify.

They were talking about the bishop and his family: at least, the engineer and Crawshaw were. Olsen was taking no part in the conversation, it was almost as if he resented it. Well, why the hell shouldn't he? He was among foreigners, standing up to the strains of that a lot better than he, MacGregor, felt that he'd be capable of doing himself, stuck indefinitely in a crowd of people who neither talked nor thought in English.

'You know –' he made sure of the effectiveness of his interruption by carelessly jolting the table as he leaned forward, so that soup slopped at the same moment as he broke into the conversation: 'You know, you'll feel pretty stupid, this time tomorrow. We'll have them here – our passengers – right *here*, flesh and blood, nice people, *brave* people. If I had a record of your bloody stupid jokes, and I played it here tomorrow night – eh?'

They looked at him, surprised. Olsen, realising that the interruption had been for him, looked up somewhere over the Captain's head, and coloured slightly in embarrassment. MacGregor ploughed on.

'I was thinking: five charges to a pattern, and say two patterns from one of those trawlers and three from the other. Ten charges, and fifteen. Well, a trawler'd carry more than that . . . '

They joined, dutifully, in the discussion. All it added up to was that nobody could fathom the reasons or the intentions in the enemy's minds. But it came to more than that, too: to the fact that Chief and Crawshaw were perfectly happy to accept the situation, the release or reprieve: and now, having swallowed that whole and with no signs of resultant indigestion, they accepted just as easily the absence of air patrols, *Setter*'s freedom to close the coast, on the surface and in daylight, without any sign of enemy interest.

MacGregor thought, hopelessly, That's it. They don't see anything, and I can't explain it, not even to myself, I only know it stinks – more strongly every minute.

.   .   .   .

Supper was over; Crawshaw went up on the bridge, and Soames came down hungry for his; Olsen put a new blade in his razor and shut himself in the tiny lavatory to remove several days' growth of beard. By the time he got back to the wardroom, Soames had worked through to the coffee stage and they were waiting to start a game of Liar Dice.

Olsen played badly, losing three match-sticks and thus his first 'life' in the first three games. MacGregor asked him, 'Something on your mind, Olsen? You were pretty sharp, last time.'

Chief's beard vibrated as he laughed. 'He's looking forward to his duties tomorrow morning, I wouldn't be surprised . . . ' He glanced quickly at the Captain, remembering too late that this was recently forbidden ground. But Olsen grinned, fingering his newly-shaved cheek.

'Quite right. Even if this girl is ugly, I am still looking forward. I will be honoured to meet her father, also. Among us Norwegian people, he is a . . . ' He shrugged, not knowing how to put it. 'He is a great man, for us.'

MacGregor held up the leather cup with the five dice in it, his palm over the top as he shook it gently. He said, 'Tell us about him, Sub.'

'Oh . . . Well, when the Germans came and occupied Norway, there were some Norwegians who received them well. I think it would be that in any country – you have your people too, in England, the 18 B – you know? Perhaps there would have been others, to join them – weak people more than bad ones. But Bishop Dalen spoke against them very strongly, in the churches, and then in churches all over Norway the priests spoke the same things. Thank you . . . ' Olsen took a cigarette from the engineer's tin. When it was lit, he went on, 'The Germans sent for him and told him that he must not say these things against the traitors who were ready to work with them. They said to him, "You must tell all the priests to stop making these speeches." Bishop Dalen say to the Germans, "I say what I say, and I do not have orders from you." The Germans let him go because they know that there will be much trouble everywhere in Norway if they do not. But Bishop Dalen goes on the same and so do all his priests and they say prayers in the churches for the men and women of the Resistance. When there are hostages taken he prays for them too, and when some hostages are murdered he makes special services for – to their memory. So another time the Germans take him away and this time he is in prison for several weeks, and many other priests are taken too. Then they let Bishop Dalen go but not all the priests; they keep them in prison or they murder them, we do not know. The Germans tell the bishop that this is his last chance, if he does any more what he has been doing they will arrest him and his family too and they will be shot, and all the churches will be closed in Norway.'

Olsen spoke quietly, looking down at his hands which were linked on the edge of the table. Occasionally he paused for a word, for the translation of Norwegian thought into English speech with limited vocabulary. Glancing up now, he saw that all their eyes were on him, their expressions thoughtful. Cigarette smoke drifted slowly upwards to wreathe around the lamp with its crude decoration of spirit-bottle labels. He shrugged, and told them, 'So now the bishop is more careful. He is more quiet and – diplomatic? – and the Germans leave him alone. But then – he could not truly stop his work, I think. He must go on, in private ways. I suppose this has happened and the Germans found it out. It must be this or he would not be wishing to leave Norway.'

Olsen stopped talking. MacGregor nodded, slowly. 'He's quite a man, your bishop. I think we'll *all* be glad to meet him . . . Look, I think it'd be a good thing for the ship's company to hear what you've been telling us – so they'll know what this is about. What d'you say, Olsen – will you give it to them over the loudspeakers, when we dive in the morning?'

'Of course, Sir. I would be glad.'

'Bloody good idea!' Chief nodded enthusiastically. 'Well – someone going to throw those dice?'

MacGregor raised the leather pot, and shook it hard, muttering an incantation for good luck: then the dice rattled down on to the table between his cupped hands, where the other players couldn't see them, and while the Captain peered at them and feigned astonishment at the wonders which he'd no doubt claim to have thrown, the engineer muttered, 'You know, Olsen, I think I *will* wash my beard. That bishop of yours deserves it.'

MacGregor set the cup down, covering the group of dice, and slid it carefully across the table to Soames, who was on his right.

'I'll go easy on you, Pilot. Three Aces. You'd be silly not to take it.'

15

BY ten o'clock, Soames had turned in; the curtains were drawn across his bunk, and gentle rhythmic snores came from behind it. But the others were still up: Olsen because he was due on watch at the half-hour – it hadn't been worth turning in, when the Liars game ended – Chief because Featherstone was still working to repair the for'ard hydroplanes, and the Captain because they were closing the enemy coast under peculiar conditions and he'd every intention of staying awake all night.

'You're clear about tomorrow, Olsen – meeting the boat?'

Olsen nodded. 'I will have the Second Cox'n and Hughes with me, Sir. I have talked with Hallet about it.'

' 'M. They'll use *this* hatch –' MacGregor jerked a thumb upwards, at the guntower hatch over their heads – 'and you'll come up behind me into the bridge. Next behind you I want the Oerlikon gunner and after them both Vickers gunners.'

Olsen looked surprised, and Chief asked, fatuously, 'Are we expecting the bishop to resist, then?'

'Don't be bloody stupid . . . ' MacGregor turned back to Olsen. 'Just in case – well, any sort of monkey business. You never know. If Gerry'd got wind of it – not that I'm suggesting it's likely – but it's just as well to be on our toes.'

Olsen began to move. 'I had better speak with McAllister, about the Oerlikon. And the Vickers –'

'Hell, leave it to the morning! After we've dived, Sub. We'll get 'em all together and brief 'em in one go, casing party and all. O.K.?'

Chief dragged himself out into the gangway and went off for'ard, no doubt to pass the time of day with Featherstone. He wanted the job on the fore 'planes finished: not only for the obvious reasons but also in order that he could turn in and get a full night's sleep. This was the last night he'd have in his own bunk, since he'd agreed to surrender it and move to a camp bed in the Control Room, to make room for the bishop's party. He could have turned in, anyway, but as his department (as represented by Featherstone) was still at work, he felt that he should himself remain awake and vertical until the job was done.

The watch messenger appeared, and looked meaningly

at Olsen. The Norwegian glanced up at the clock: ten-twenty. 'Thank you – it's all right.' He nodded, and the messenger went back to the Control Room. Olsen extricated himself from behind the table, and got his Ursula suit out from the hooks at the back of the bulkhead door. When he'd buttoned and zipped the dun-coloured waterproof suit he took his binoculars out of their case, cleaned the glasses at each end and turned the adjustment to the right setting for his own eyesight.

'Are you not turning in, Sir?'

MacGregor shook his head. 'Not yet awhile. I may come up and keep you company, presently.'

Olsen went into the Control Room. Catching the helmsman's eye, he pointed to the hatch, and the helmsman yelled into the voicepipe. 'Bridge! Relieve officer of the watch, please Sir?'

Crawshaw's voice floated out of the tube. 'Yes, please.' Olsen was already on the ladder, climbing up.

The air was sharply cold, sticky with salt dampness, and the sea was a pearly grey under pale, filtered sunlight. Three seagulls drifted overhead, their great wings spread and tiny, sharp-beaked heads jerking from side to side as they watched suspiciously or greedily for Lord knew what. The diesels rumbled steadily, leaving a double trail of brownish exhaust which drifted back over the submarine's broad, white wake, and above the noise of the engines was the sound of the sea itself as it rushed aft, foaming, along the saddle-tanks, swirled across the pressure-hull below the platform of the bridge.

Olsen stepped up beside Crawshaw. 'Hello.'

Crawshaw said, 'You're in good time, this evening. What is it – insomnia?'

'Please?'

'Couldn't you sleep?'

'Oh. We were playing Liars. There was not time enough for a sleep. Only Soames is asleep, now.'

'What an extraordinary thing. Well – you ready to take over? Course oh-nine-oh. Four-two-oh revs. At midnight, reduce to three-six-oh revs and put on a running charge both sides. I'll tell 'em downstairs to remind you of that, at midnight. O.K.?'

'O.K.' Olsen had been sweeping the horizon through his binoculars; now he lowered them, and took a quick look round the bridge. The two lookouts were hard at it, sweeping as steadily as machines. Keeping an efficient lookout was something which submariners could have taught the rest of the Navy a great deal about. He told Crawshaw, 'All right. Sleep well.'

The First Lieutenant went below, leaving *Setter* in Olsen's hands, and Olsen felt, as always, that strange and hardly describable thrill which had already made him heart and soul a submariner. It was this feeling of isolation, in enemy territory; the immense surrounding of hostile sea and sky, the deadly purpose of the submarine herself beneath his feet and in his hands. Sleek and gleaming, she was not a ship that carried weapons, so much as a weapon herself: a creature of the sea, lethal and loaded, vicious and designed only for destruction: he took the glasses from his eyes and looked down for a moment at the long, wet line of her, the snake-like head that was her bow as it smashed and lanced a gleaming road through the gentle, oily swell: and he thought – or perhaps *felt*, because it was his heart and his emotions that were stirred – that in all his life he had never set eyes on anything even half as beautiful.

.   .   .   .

MacGregor came up on the bridge soon after Olsen had taken over. He leant against the for'ard periscope standard, behind Olsen – and below him, because there was a raised step in the front of the bridge. So when the Norwegian swept round with his binoculars, he looked clear over the Captain's head instead of meeting an interruption in his steady, continuous search.

MacGregor used his glasses, now and then, but most of the time he just leant there, watching the sea rush past: Olsen, glancing back at him in the pauses when he had to stop and wipe the sea dew off the lenses of the binoculars, wondered if this Scotsman loved the sight and sound and feel of it as much as he did himself. It wasn't a thing you could talk to people about, or explain: it was a subtle, private pleasure, almost a mood.

Presumably MacGregor enjoyed it: since he was up here of his own free will and could, if he'd wanted, have been comfortably asleep in his bunk.

Neither of them spoke, although the Captain was up there for more than an hour. Then, just before midnight, the helmsman called up for permission for the first of the relief lookouts to come up and take over, and MacGregor, hearing it, said, 'Tell 'em to wait a minute, Sub. I'm going down.' He lowered himself into the hatch and Olsen told the helmsman, 'Wait – Captain coming down.'

'Aye aye, Sir.'

Then the first relief came up, and the man who'd been relieved went down, and the helmsman called again, 'Permission to relieve second lookout?'

'Yes.'

'And, bridge?'

'Bridge.'

'Twelve o'clock, Sir.'

'Very good . . . Three-six-oh revolutions, running charge port and starboard.'

The tempo of the diesels' pounding slowed: *Setter*'s bow sagged lower in the water, and the bow-wave and the wake narrowed as her speed fell off.

'Bridge!'

'Bridge.'

'Helmsman relieved, Sir. Course oh-nine-oh, three-six-oh revs, running charge both sides.'

'Very good.'

Twenty minutes later, a bleary-eyed Soames struggled out of the hatch, yawning and shivering. 'Lord, but it's cold!'

Olsen told him, 'Perhaps you have too many blankets on your bunk. *I* am not cold.'

'Perhaps *you* have cold blood in your veins, coming from where you do. I'm from sunny Surrey, myself.'

'It is a nice place, that one?'

'It's all right . . . You want me to take over now, or d'you like it too much up here?'

'You can have it, for a bit. Course oh-nine-oh, three-sixty revs, running charge both sides. That's all.'

Soames stepped up to the front of the bridge, raising his binoculars. 'How many U-boats in sight this morning?'

'Only three or four. Here – there – *you* know.'

'That's all right, then . . . Goodnight.'

When Olsen got down below, he found MacGregor working at the chart table. He'd got out the large-scale chart and he'd marked the rendezvous position on it, and now he was studying the coastlines of Vikna and Leka Islands, and the depth soundings. Olsen squeezed past him into the wardroom, and at the same moment the Cox'n appeared from the direction of the galley, carrying two steaming mugs of cocoa.

146

'Captain, Sir – kye? Mr Olsen – kye for you?'

'Cox'n, you're a bloody marvel!' MacGregor took his mug and set it on the edge of the chart table. Olsen, seeing the clouds of steam rising, realised that it would be ten minutes before it was cool enough to drink, and that was ten minutes' sleep gone. The Cox'n, as if he'd read his thoughts, murmured, 'Lay you out, Sir, that will.'

MacGregor glanced round sharply, meeting a bland, innocent stare from Chief Petty Officer Bird. Leaning forward, he sniffed at the cocoa-steam.

'Cox'n . . . there's rum, in this.'

'*Rum*, Sir?' It seemed the Cox'n had never heard the word before, there was such bewilderment in his expression. Olsen sniffed at his own mug: it was rum, all right, not a doubt of it.

The Captain was staring hard at Bird. 'Yes, Cox'n. Rum, in my kye. And in Sub-Lieutenant Olsen's too, judging by the way he's licking his lips.'

The Cox'n scratched his chin. 'Well, Sir, if that's so, then there must've been rum in them mugs, earlier on like, and some lazy bastard didn't wash 'em out proper. That's the only thing *I* can think of, Sir . . . Shall I get you a couple o' fresh cups, Sir – chuck that lot out?'

MacGregor, smiled, and shook his head. 'These'll do, Cox'n . . . Thank you.'

'You're welcome, Sir.'

While they were drinking it, Chief arrived from up for'ard: he wore a fresh coating of oil and grease. He told the Captain, ''Planes are O.K., now. Featherstone's just finishing off, but they're all right. He'll put 'em back in normal control right away.'

'That's good news, Chief. What was the matter with 'em?'

'If you want a word for it – thrombosis . . . Is there any more of that kye, anywhere? Eh?'

MacGregor pointed towards the Control Room. 'Ask the Cox'n. Tell him you want Four Star.'

.   .   .   .

Bird had been right about the soporific qualities of the laced cocoa: Olsen was unconscious within seconds of getting into his bunk. Fading out of awareness into a heavy, dreamless sleep, the warmth of the cocoa and the fire of the rum enveloped him in a soft cloud of utter relaxation: he drifted warmly, feeling the paralysis steal through his limbs and blanket his mind: then – it seemed like ten minutes later – he was brought abruptly to the surface by a hand which had grasped his shoulder and now was shaking it while a voice intoned in dreary, mumbled repetition, 'Four-fifteen Mr Olsen, time f'yer watch, four-fifteen, Mr Ol –'

'All right!' Sitting up and swinging his legs over the side of the bunk, peering down into the darkened ward-room, he was filled momentarily with an intense dislike for all ships, all sailors, all Englishmen: this ship and these men in particular. Then memory seeped in to remind him that today, this very morning, they'd be meeting the bishop and his family. So it wasn't such a bad day, after all. In fact he was looking forward to it, and he didn't mind, now, getting dressed and going up to relieve Crawshaw.

He climbed down into the wardroom and sat on the end of the bench to drag on the trousers of an Ursula suit, and while he was doing it MacGregor came down from the bridge.

'G' morning, Sir.'

'Well, Olsen. That rum do you good?'

'I slept very well.' Olsen shook his head. '*Too* well, I think now.'

MacGregor nodded. 'I had an hour or so, myself.'

'Everything is all right, Sir? The same?'

'The same. Except that we're getting closer in every minute. Keep your eyes open, up there, Sub.'

'Yes.' Olsen slid his arms into the jacket, grabbed his binoculars and went into the Control Room. He was thinking that the Captain was looking washed-out, tired and worried. The Norwegian couldn't see any reason for such tension in the man, and it seemed to him that as they'd be having a busy day with their guests, first meeting them and then looking after them, getting them settled in, the Captain would have shown more sense if he'd got himself a night's sleep.

But twenty minutes later MacGregor appeared on the bridge again, leaning in exactly the same place against the periscope standard, watching the gulls which floated overhead and astern, swooping low over the wake and screaming in wild, mad voices: the voices, so they said, of drowned sailors . . . Olsen thought that MacGregor must be worrying about something which he was keeping to himself: but surely, when all these hours had gone by without sight or sound of an enemy aircraft, without any interruption at all, he could have relaxed, and slept? After all, most patrols were spent a lot closer to enemy coasts than *Setter* was now . . . The Captain's continuous presence had become an annoyance, a suggestion that he didn't trust the efficiency of the officer of the watch . . .

'Bridge!'

He stooped to the voicepipe. 'Bridge.'

'Would you tell the Captain, Sir – signal coming through, addressed to us.'

Olsen straightened, and turned to pass the message, but MacGregor was already climbing down into the hatch. As

149

his head disappeared, he shouted, 'All right, Sub. I heard.'

Olsen thought, He was so quick off the mark, you could almost think he'd been waiting for it!

.   .   .   .

Chief came grumbling out of his bunk like a sick bear out of its cave.

'God, what a night! I ask you – half an hour's bloody sleep and now *this*!'

'Nonsense, Chief. You've had all of four hours, which is a damn sight more than anyone else gets, in a row. Come on – this is urgent.' MacGregor had brought the cipher books out of the safe himself, and he had them ready on the wardroom table. 'Ready, Chief?'

The engineer pulled the heavy books towards him across the table. He snapped irritably, 'All right. I'm ready.' His tone implied, 'Let's get the bloody thing done with!'

MacGregor read the groups out and as the engineer translated them he scrawled the message in blue pencil on a pink signal pad. The first words were *Do not repeat NOT attempt carry out previous orders but proceed seawards immediately stop –*

Chief was waiting to look up the next group of cipher, but MacGregor jumped to his feet. 'Hang on, Chief . . . ' He went into the Control Room, and called up the voice-pipe to Olsen, 'Bridge!'

Olsen recognised the voice. 'Sir?'

'Come round to two-seven-oh, Sub.'

By the time MacGregor was back in the wardroom, *Setter* was under helm, reversing her course: they heard the helmsman's report, 'Twenty of starboard wheel on, Sir!'

'O.K., Chief. Let's get on with it.'

'You look pleased.'

'I am. Something *had* to be wrong . . . Now, next group –'

The rest of the message read, *New rendezvous at* 0700/22 *in position* 65 *degrees* 50 *minutes north* 11 *degrees* 20 *minutes east stop Boat will fly white flag and red sweater.*

The Captain sat back, staring at the engineer. 'They cut *that* pretty fine, didn't they? We might've been dived, by now, and then we wouldn't have got it.'

Chief yawned; he took MacGregor's scrawled translation of the cipher, and peered at it. 'Where's this new position? If we've got to be there at seven tomorrow morning –'

'It's not far . . . Let's check this through again, Chief. I'll take the book and you read out.'

They worked through the message again and got the same answers. MacGregor stood up, and turned to the chart table, and Chief crawled silently back into his bunk.

The new position certainly wasn't far. About forty-five miles from the first one, it was just north west of Vega Island. So the bishop and his party would presumably be pushing off from Vega instead of from Leka. MacGregor had two thoughts about it: first, that he'd have been happier if the new rendezvous had been a bit farther away from the first one, and second that the Germans must have been pretty close on the old boy's heels, to have forced such a last-minute change in plans.

The messenger came and told him, 'From the officer of the watch, Sir: course now two-seven-oh.'

'Very good.' MacGregor wondered what sort of reception *Setter* would have run into, if they hadn't been on the surface to get this signal in time to be turned about. The words *proceed seawards immediately* clearly indicated trouble waiting inshore. He thought, I'll stay on the surface for a couple of hours, to get out a bit and to get the battery properly charged. Then we'll dive, and, please God, have a nice, quiet day . . . *Sleep!*

It occurred to him that Olsen, up there on the bridge, would know nothing yet except that they'd turned their backs on the rendezvous position. The lad'd be having kittens worrying about his bishop. MacGregor smiled to himself, and headed for the ladder.

. . . .

The Captain had turned in, and left orders to be shaken at seven o'clock: at five past he appeared on the bridge with a sextant and took some sights on the North Star. It was the only visible object and while observations of it alone couldn't give them a fix, it would give an accurate latitude which would be a lot better than nothing. He took three or four sights, shouting down the sextant readings to the man he'd stationed down below to record the times of the sights by the deck-watch. When MacGregor was satisfied, he said, 'Down you go, lookouts.' The two men jumped for the hatch, and the Captain handed the sextant to Soames. 'You go down, too, Sub. You can start working out those sights.'

'Aye aye, Sir.' Holding the sextant carefully against his chest so as to be sure of not giving it a knock on the rim of the hatch, Soames climbed one-handed down into the Control Room. The Petty Officer of the watch asked him, 'We diving, Sir?' Soames shrugged: MacGregor hadn't said anything. He went for'ard to the chart table, murmuring, 'I suppose so.'

The klaxon roared twice: and that was the answer. The diesels stopped, making a strange and sudden silence as the last cough of the klaxon died: the vents dropped open as the

E.R.A. on watch snatched at the levers on the control panel: there was a rush of feet and men cursing and Chief passed by with his eyes shut: the top hatch slammed shut over MacGregor's head as *Setter* wallowed down into the sea. MacGregor, pushing the pins into the clips on the underside of the hatch, yelled down, 'Sixty feet, Number One!'

'Sixty feet, Sir!'

By now, every man was in his place, and the noise and the rush was over. The needles swung fast around the gauges and at forty feet Crawshaw said, 'Blow Q.'

'Blow Q, Sir.' Featherstone wrenched the valve open, and the rate of dive lessened, the angle decreasing as the submarine approached her ordered depth. Crawshaw asked the Captain, as he stepped off the ladder, 'Vent Q inboard, Sir?'

MacGregor thought for a moment . . . 'No – outboard.' There weren't any aircraft about, to see the bubble when it was released, and as he was planning to make it a long day dived he didn't want all that extra pressure in the submarine's atmosphere. Crawshaw told Featherstone, 'Vent Q outboard.' A minute later, the boat was steady at sixty feet.

'Slow together.'

'Slow ahead together, Sir.'

MacGregor told Crawshaw, 'Stop one motor when you've caught the trim. We'll stay at this depth.' Then he reached up, and took the microphone off its hook.

'D'you hear, there? Gather round the loudspeakers, and listen . . . '

He told them about the signal, the change in plans and the new rendezvous for seven o'clock on the following morning. Then he paused, and went on: 'Now, this

Bishop Dalen. You may be wondering who he is, and why we've been sent to get him and his family out of Norway. Anyway, they'll be our guests for several days, so I think we should all know a bit about him. Sub-Lieutenant Olsen – as you know, he's Norwegian – is going to tell you now what sort of a bishop this is . . . Here, Olsen. Tell 'em what you told me last night, will you?'

Olsen stammered a bit, at first, being unused to the microphone and selfconscious with all the men in the Control Room watching his face as he talked. But he settled down to it quickly and added a few points which he'd remembered during the night. It was clear from the way he told the story that he wanted *Setter*'s ship's company to share his own admiration for Bishop Dalen. When he'd finished, he handed the grey, palm-sized microphone back to Mac-Gregor. 'Thank you, Sir.'

MacGregor wound up the speeches for the morning. 'Well, now you know. Quite a man, this bishop, isn't he? So you'll see to it – every one of you – that he and his family enjoy their time with us . . . That's all. Watch Diving.'

In the gangway by the wardroom, Ellis came up to Olsen and spoke confidentially. 'That bishop, Sir. You reckon he likes a drop o' rum?'

Olsen hesitated, surprised at the question. 'Oh – I should think yes, he would, Ellis.'

'Ah.' The messman looked pleased. 'Then tomorrow night, 'e can 'ave me tot.'

16

KJELLEGARD said, 'Almost at once. But first I must have one hour's sleep. That, and a bite to eat – Anna, you've some bread, or something?'

The bishop told him, 'She's given us a most excellent breakfast. Porridge, fish, and milk. We're positively bloated!'

Anna laughed. 'There's some left for you, and the menu is unchanged. Do you want to eat now, or when you wake up?'

'Now, I think, if it's ready. But if it'll take long, then I'll sleep first and you can wake me when you've got it done. Where are the Vikens?'

'Away for two days. When they come back, if the Germans are here, they'll find the lock broken on the front door and that's all they'll know.' She smiled at Kjellegard. 'This was my idea and they agreed to it ... I'll give you your meal now and you can sleep after it.'

'Good! I can use the Vikens' bedroom, and really stretch out. What luxury!'

'You can't, I'm afraid.' The bishop spoke apologetically. 'My wife and Kari are sleeping there.' He pointed at the long, sagging sofa. 'You could use that. Anna and I'll sit in the kitchen so you won't be disturbed ... Did you get your message off?'

Kjellegard nodded. 'Yes. I only hope it will have got back to the submarine in time . . . that most *unfortunate* submarine!'

The bishop raised his eyebrows. 'How, unfortunate?' Anna called from the kitchen at the same time, 'Come on! Porridge is hot!' Kjellegard moved stiffly across the room. He said, 'They're so hot on our trail that we – Anna and I – will have to go with you. You can't sail the boat out on your own, and we can't take you out and then return – as we would have done – because it's most unlikely we'd be able to land unobserved and get away. And – oh, that smells delicious!' He sat down stiffly at the kitchen table, groaning as his bottom touched the chair.

Anna laughed. 'My bicycle?'

'Is that what you call it? . . . Well, I shouldn't be rude about it, I suppose – it's served its purpose. But it's an instrument of torture, more than a bicycle . . . '

Between mouthfuls of the thick, steaming porridge, he went on with what he'd been telling the bishop:

'I was saying, in there . . . I can't allow the Vikens to take you out – they'd be arrested the minute they landed. Anyway, they aren't here, now. But the Germans aren't all fools, unfortunately. So Anna and I will take you, and go with you in the submarine, and we'll leave the boat to drift. It isn't the Vikens' boat, it came from up north of here, and its owners know nothing except they've lost it. By now they'll have reported it as stolen, I dare say. It'll be found drifting, that's all.'

Anna was staring at Kjellegard as he ate and talked: she had slices of fish frying in a pan and she was poking at it from time to time with a flat, spoonlike instrument, but her eyes stayed on Kjellegard. She murmured, 'To *England*, then? *Me?*'

Kjellegard nodded, scraping the last of the porridge off his plate. The bishop asked her, gently, 'Have you any family, people who'll miss you?'

Kjellegard grunted, and pushed his plate across the table. He answered for her. 'She had a brother. The Germans shot him.'

Anna put the plate of fish down in front of Kjellegard, and told the bishop, 'He was in a group of hostages. They shot them in the square, in public. I was there . . . Milk?'

'Thank you. You're a wonderful cook, Anna.'

'You should thank the Vikens. They had it prepared for us. . . . Will they be all right, the Vikens?'

'Why not? We'll leave no traces here. Why should the Germans come to this farm, rather than to any other?' Kjellegard gulped down the last of the fish, and drank the milk in one long swallow. 'I eat like a pig, Bishop. Excuse me. I was hungry.'

The bishop chuckled. 'You can eat like fifty pigs, for all I care. How long shall we leave you to sleep – an hour, did you say?'

'Exactly one hour, please. Have all of you ready, then, so we can leave at once when you wake me . . . Anna, that was a marvellous meal. Thank you.' He half rose, but groaned loudly and sank back on to the chair. Anna and the bishop laughed as they took his elbows and hauled him up.

'It's all very well, you laughing. But if I'm crippled – paralysed – I won't be much use to you!' He hobbled to the door. 'Oh, that bicycle!'

Anna asked him, 'What shall we do with it? Give it to the Vikens?'

'I wouldn't give it to my worst enemy . . . No, Anna. The Germans might have a report soon, on my own journey, and then if they found the thing here the Vikens would most certainly be shot. No, we'll take it with us, and drop it overboard.' He nodded, warming to the idea. 'I would like the privilege of doing that personally.'

They shut the door behind him so that there'd be no disturbance to his short rest in the little parlour. Anna began to collect the plates, to wash up, and the bishop picked up a dish-cloth.

'I'll dry.'

She turned a horrified face to him. 'No, Bishop! Certainly, you must not! In any case, two plates and one cup is – and in any case, *no*!'

The bishop smiled, 'Come along. Don't keep the staff waiting.'

'Bishop – I think, if I may suggest it, you should go up to wake Mrs Dalen and Kari. They will need time to prepare themselves: women don't like to jump out of bed and rush straight out. You could take a jug of milk up with you, if you like. There's plenty left.'

'Very good advice, Anna. I'll do it – when we've cleared up these dishes.'

. . . .

Mrs Dalen was sitting in a chair by the window. When her husband put his head round the door, she raised a finger to her lips and pointed at the bed where Kari lay asleep. The bishop came into the room, a jug of milk in one hand and two cups in the other: he pushed the door shut by leaning back against it.

'She will have to wake up, my dear. We're on the move again, in less than an hour. Anna thought you might like a drink of milk.'

'She is a nice person, that Anna.'

'Yes.' He set the jug and cups down on the wash-stand. 'She can't be more than a year or two older than Kari, but – well, I think she's had a rough time of it. She's a *woman*, if you know what I mean.'

'Kari's still a baby. And isn't *she* going through enough?'

'Oh, yes. But she doesn't truly feel it, probably because she has us with her, to take the decisions and for her to cry to when she is unhappy. This girl Anna – she told me they shot her brother. One of the reprisal murders, I gathered. She's coming with us, by the way … Are you going to wake Kari?'

'Anna is coming with us? To England?'

'Yes. And my friend Kjellegard, too. It is necessary, for various reasons. If they stayed behind, they would almost certainly be arrested.'

'I hope there'll be room for them, in the submarine?'

'There'll have to be. And I don't suppose it takes long, from here to Scotland. *Do* wake that girl.'

Mrs Dalen crossed the room and sat on the edge of the bed, beside her daughter. She put her hand on the raised shoulder, and patted it gently. 'Kari, wake up. It's time to be up, darling.'

The girl twisted over on her back, and gazed sleepily about the room. Her eyes were a clear, bright blue under the tangle of yellow hair. I've only been drowsing. I heard what you said. It's nice they're coming, I think.'

The bishop poured milk into the cups. 'We've got about half an hour. Then we go down to the beach, to the fjord, and we cross over to Vega in a motorboat of some sort. Kjellegard tells me the sea's quite flat, so you needn't be worried about seasickness or anything of that sort.'

'He's nice.' Kari sat up, smiling as she pushed the hair back off her face. 'I'm glad he's coming to England . . . I don't like foreigners.'

The bishop frowned slightly. 'British people are very like us, Kari. We have a great deal in common with them. And in any case, there are thousands of Norwegians over there, whom you will meet.'

159

'I don't need *thousands*. But – foreigners – well, the Swedes are like us, aren't they? In many ways? But that hasn't stopped them letting German troops through to attack us, has it?'

The bishop told her. 'You'd better start getting ready, Kari, instead of talking about things you don't understand. As to Kjellegard – well, he's an excellent chap, but he's well over forty and you're a child of nineteen.'

'I wouldn't mind if he was ninety – I'd *still* like him!' She saw the jug. 'Is that something to drink?' Kari got up off the bed, and stretched, and the bishop thought, Nineteen – yes. Child – hardly! He told her, 'Yes. Milk.' He picked up one of the cups and took it over to his wife. 'Here. Do you good . . . Now, I was explaining to you. We cross over to the island, to Vega, and the motorboat leaves us there and goes on to wherever it's going. Then we go right across the island and get into a different boat – a *Redningsskøyte* – for the last stage of this journey. We'll be all together all the time, so you'll have nothing to worry about.'

Kari crossed the room and took the other cup. 'What is a *Redningsskøyte*, Father?'

'A big sort of sailing boat. A lifeboat, really. They have to be very strongly built because sometimes they spend all the winter months at sea. That's what Kjellegard told me.'

'Is he a sailor, then?'

Mrs Dalen glanced reproachfully at her husband. She had plainly decided that the name Kjellegard was one to be avoided. The bishop told his daughter, 'No. He was in the Army . . . Well, I'll go down.' He looked at his watch. 'Please don't be long.'

Anna was sitting at the kitchen table, reading some old newspapers. The bishop came in and closed the door: he said, 'Ten minutes. Then I must wake him.'

160

She pushed the papers aside. 'I will have to learn English now.'

'You don't know any?'

'Oh – what they taught us at school. But not enough to read the newspapers properly. But I was thinking – there will be *real* papers there, with truth in them! Instead of all this rubbish about the Germans winning all their battles and all the world loving them so dearly. It makes me sick to read it . . . Would you like some more porridge, before we go?'

'No, thank you. I've had plenty to eat. You've looked after us wonderfully, Anna.'

'I've a loaf of bread, quite a big one, but I want to take it with us. On the island there may be nowhere to get food. But it's only for one day, so even if there's absolutely nothing this loaf will see us through, don't you think?'

He nodded. 'We'll have excellent food, I expect, in the British submarine. Sailors like to eat, you know!'

'Oh. I was wondering about the submarine. It's a bit frightening, that. Have you ever seen one, Bishop?'

'No, I haven't. But you shouldn't worry, Anna. It's perfectly safe. And in only two or three days we'll be on dry land again – in a free country!'

'A free country. Yes. The British are lucky, aren't they?'

'Lucky? Yes, for that – for not having Germans there. But they've had defeats and the German U-boats have kept them not far above starvation. They're lucky, I suppose, but it's not *all* luck.'

'In one thing I think they are very lucky, Bishop.' Anna smiled as she said it. The bishop asked her, 'You mean, their English Channel?'

'Oh, that. Yes. But I was thinking, they are most lucky because Scotland is not inhabited by *Swedes*.'

161

The bishop pushed back his chair, and stood up. 'You're as bad as my daughter, Anna. She has a fixation about Swedes, too . . . They're coming down, by the sound of it.' He glanced at his watch. 'I'll wake poor Kjellegard.'

Dalen went into the parlour, and closed the door behind him. The click of the latch was certainly not a loud noise, yet it brought Kjellegard wide awake at once, twisting up into a half-sitting position: his right hand vanished into the folds of his heavy, woollen jacket.

'It's all right, Kjellegard. You don't have to shoot me.'

'Ah.' The man relaxed, taking his hand off the butt of the Luger which he wore strapped against his side. It had belonged to a German officer whose throat he'd cut, one night in an Oslo suburb.

He ran a hand over his face as he stood up. 'I'm terribly stiff: it hurts all over, and worst of all, *here*. But I dare say it'll wear off . . . I wish I'd had time for a shave, too. The British are so correct, always, and their Navy, specially, has a reputation for being – what do they call it, "spick and span"?'

The bishop told him, 'I doubt if they'll mind, under the circumstances. But anyhow, I've a razor in my pack, and if there's time on the island, or even in the *Redningsskøyte*, you may certainly use it. I agree with you that we should try to look our best.'

17

THE day was a peaceful one: they spent the whole of it at sixty feet, relying on the Asdics to provide warning of any enemy: the thing to dread was the return of those A/S trawlers. If aircraft passed near, or over – well, they passed: MacGregor had no wish to see them or even to know if the Germans were searching. All *Setter* had to do was to keep out of sight and get to the new rendezvous position at the appointed time. Until then, it was more than ever essential that the enemy should have no inkling of *Setter*'s position or course. They must have known something of the first rendezvous plans, but there was no reason to believe that they'd have similar knowledge of the new ones, and if they caught a glimpse of the submarine, if some patrolling or searching aircraft spotted the white feather of a periscope's track through the water even for a second – for long enough even to wonder and yet be unsure when it vanished again – just that fleeting glimpse alone might give the game away. The hunt would be whistled up, the aircraft and the anti-submarine craft, even destroyers out of Trondheim: the coast would be patrolled and even if *Setter* herself were not detected, the bishop and his party would have no chance to move.

So today it was sixty feet, slow ahead on one motor and orders to keep as quiet as possible. The batteries had been fully charged when they dived, and MacGregor intended to surface for the shortest possible time this evening, to top them up against whatever demands might be made on them during the next day, and to get some fresh air into the boat. Then he'd dive and stay under water until he had the white flag and the red sweater in the calibrated circle of the periscope.

MacGregor himself slept most of the day, only getting out of his bunk for meals and for a quick check on the Control Room, then turning in again in deep, warm silence as the waiting day drew on.

Everything was ready for the visitors. The Ladies'

Boudoir had its canvas screen rigged, and it had been tested carefully for visibility, or privacy, with the T.I. acting as a model, from all angles. The Cox'n had checked his stores, and he'd selected some of the less revolting canned food for the guests' first meals. After the first day, he reckoned, they'd be used to it. MacGregor had opened the wine locker in one of the less accessible corners of the wardroom: it had involved moving a lot of carefully stowed gear and putting it back again after he'd taken what he wanted out of the locker, which was a bottle of whisky for the bishop and one of sherry for the female passengers. He'd put them at the back of his personal drawer, where he could get at them quickly when the time came.

Olsen, on sudden impulse, had gone into the wardroom W.C. to check on his carefully written instructions regarding the operation of that mechanism. As he'd expected, the sheet of signal pad was crumpled and dirty: his brother officers had spent certain periods trying to decipher the Norwegian words. So he wrote it all out again on a clean sheet of paper.

Just after lunch, Crawshaw asked the Captain, 'What about the swear-boxes, Sir? Hadn't we better take them down? The bishop might wonder what they were for, and it'd be tricky to explain. D'you think?'

MacGregor pressed the bell for the Control Room messenger. When the man came, he told him, 'Ask the Cox'n to come and see me, if he's finished his lunch.'

'Aye aye, Sir.'

'You're right, Number One. I think they've served their purpose.'

Chief grinned, over a clean beard. 'You won't believe this. When Featherstone was working on the 'planes, last night – and he'd been at it for bloody hours, too – he dropped a damn great wrench on his bad foot, and he didn't say a thing! Featherstone, of all people!'

When the Cox'n came aft, MacGregor told him, 'Cox'n, I want the swear-boxes brought in here, now. And I want all members of the Canteen Committee present to witness the money counted.'

'Aye aye, Sir.' Bird turned to go. Then he stopped. 'But some of 'em are on watch, Sir.'

'Get the ones who aren't.'

The boxes were lined up on the wardroom table, and, under the eyes of the First Lieutenant (who was Treasurer of the committee), the Cox'n, the Petty Officer Telegraphist, Leading Seaman Hallet, Stoker Mason and Able Seaman Green, MacGregor counted the money. It came to four pounds, seven shillings.

'You all satisfied with that count?'

They were. The Cox'n asked, 'What are you going to do with it, Sir?'

'Put it in the Canteen Fund, of course.' There were smiles all round. Stoker Mason, always a man for a party, asked, 'Ship's Company Run, Sir?'

'Why not? But it's up to your committee. You can do what the hell you like with it . . . Number One, you'll take charge of this cash, now.'

'Right, Sir.'

The Petty Officer Telegraphist asked, 'Can we carry on swearing, now, Sir?'

'No, you bloody well can't!'

The Canteen Fund was a communal fund used for many purposes, but perhaps the most popular of them was an occasional party known as a Ship's Company Run Ashore. Usually they took a room in a pub, a day or two before sailing for patrol, and the fund paid for the beer. There'd be a piano in the room, and someone who could play it, and a few of the lads would bring their girl friends. There was often a fight or two, towards the end of the evening, but everyone enjoyed it and MacGregor himself had never been known to miss one.

.   .   .   .

Setter surfaced at eight that evening, and dived again at midnight. MacGregor turned her in towards the coast: he'd got a fairly good fix off a couple of planets and the North Star, and there was plenty of time in hand. He took the submarine down to sixty feet again, and when she was steady there he ordered 'Watch Diving.' Olsen took over the Control Room watch from Crawshaw, happily aware that in next to no time Soames would be in to take over from him.

MacGregor called the Cox'n, Chef and Ellis into the wardroom.

'Assuming we meet our Norwegian friends on schedule, at seven, it's reasonable to think that we'll be dived and clear away by eight. So I want breakfast then – at eight o'clock. All right?'

The Cox'n nodded. 'Aye aye, Sir.'

MacGregor turned to the cook. 'What have you got for 'em, Chef? Their first meal's got to be good.'

Bird broke in again. 'I've got it in 'and, Sir. I've got the stores up, and Chef 'ere's got the menu.' He ticked the items off on his fingers as he announced them. 'Start: corn flakes. Pusser's milk. Next, powdered egg, bacon and tomato, served on toast. Then bread and marmalade. Coffee.' He looked at the Captain. 'You wouldn't do better in the Ritz, Sir.'

'It'll do. But toast, not bread, for the passengers. And not *burnt* toast, Chef.'

'Aye aye, Sir.'

'And one other thing. How d'you make coffee, usually?'

'Well, Sir – well –' The Chef looked round, as if for help. All he got were hard, unsympathetic stares. 'Well, Sir, I just brews it up, like.'

'Quite . . . Well, Chef, the Cox'n will now give you a personal demonstration of how to make coffee that *tastes* of coffee. And as from now, that's the way you'll make it. I want four cups of it in here in ten minutes' time, as samples.'

'Aye aye, Sir.' The Cox'n practically frogmarched the cook into his galley. When the coffee arrived, it wasn't at all bad; it was certainly the nearest thing to good coffee they'd ever drunk in *Setter*. They sat round the table, enjoying it, and MacGregor muttered, 'Why the hell didn't I ever do that before?'

.   .   .   .

When Olsen turned out at four-fifteen, to take over his watch at half past, he was so filled with excitement that his fingers trembled as he knotted the laces of his canvas shoes. This was the day, and by the end of his two hours' watch it would be almost the hour! The feeling of anticipation was rather like the hour or two before a very special party: you had everything ready, the drinks out, the snacks made, the ashtrays strategically placed. You shaved, and chose a tie with care: perhaps you had a quick one before the crowd came, and you hoped that she'd arrive a bit ahead of the rush . . .

She . . . He told himself not to be a bloody fool. It was enough that he'd be meeting his countrymen, among them the famous and respected Bishop Dalen. For heaven's sake, forget the adolescent imagery! He'd have to lift the child out of the boat, as likely as not: or, if she was big enough to jump the gap, she'd be a stout, strong woman with a face like a side of beef.

Crawshaw nodded at him. 'Morning, Olsen. Thank God for a man who relieves on time. Henning's a nice chap, but he was never less than five minutes late on watch. You fit for the day?'

Olsen grinned. 'Fit as all hell.'

The First Lieutenant looked surprised. 'Your English is improving, Olsen. If that's the word for it. Tell me, do all Norwegians talk English?'

'Most. It is taught in all our schools.'

'Ah. Then I'll be able to talk to her, all right.'

'Her?'

'The bishop's daughter.'

'Oh. Yes, of course.' He thought, I've got the edge on you there, boy. The language of love doesn't need any words – but crikey, they help it along . . . He glanced at the depth-gauges. 'Shall I take over?'

'Do. Sixty feet. Starboard motor slow ahead, grouped down, port motor stopped. There's a trickle, still on the port shaft gland, so try not to use that one if you can help it. Rather go half ahead starboard than slow ahead both. OK?' Olsen nodded. Crawshaw told him, 'Course oh-eight-five. The trim's dead right and everything's shut. Captain wants a call at five. That's the lot.'

'Right. I've got it, thank you.'

'Don't forget to shake the Captain.' Crawshaw went off to his bunk, leaving Olsen alone with the watch and, under these conditions with *Setter* too deep for the periscope to be used, with practically nothing to do.

He felt as if he'd got ready for the party too early. Dressed, and the room all rigged, but two hours to kill. If you weren't careful you'd start giving yourself little drinks to help the time go by, and then you'd be tight before the party started.

He moved round to the port side of the ladder, behind the 'planesmen: watching the trim carefully, he noticed that most of the time the for'ard 'planes were carrying a few degrees of dive. A few pints of water into 'A' tank would fix that. He reached up to the electric telegraph over his head, turned the knobbed switch to *Open A*. When the watchkeeper in the for'ard compartment had opened the valve on the tank, the green light came on behind the words *A Open*. Olsen turned the pump telegraph to *Flood for'd*: he let the water run for ten seconds, then switched *Stop* and flashed to the man for'ard, *Shut A*.

Both sets of 'planes were exactly horizontal. He'd improved on Crawshaw's trim. The trouble was, there was nothing else to do now until five o'clock, when he could break the monotony by shaking MacGregor. Perhaps then the Captain would decide to come up to periscope depth, and the time would pass more quickly.

.   .   .   .

Setter was at Diving Stations. The hands of the electric clocks showed ten minutes to seven: the needles in the depth-gauges hung at thirty feet: the telegraphs were at slow ahead and the helmsman's steering indicator showed that the course was oh-eight-five. MacGregor was hunched at the big periscope, sweeping slowly round, sunlight reflected through the lenses making his eyes shine like a cat's. In the corner, Hutchins swept round too, with his Asdics, sweeping as carefully and as methodically as the Captain, only using his ears instead of his eyes.

Olsen's heart was pounding and his palms were wet. He leant against the Fruit Machine and he thought, This is worse than an attack, worse almost than being depth-charged! It was the climax of all the waiting, all the hoping, all the near-disaster: now, to meet or not to meet . . .

Suddenly the Captain stiffened, gulped air before he spoke. 'Twenty-eight feet, Number One. I can see her masts.'

'Twenty-eight feet, Sir.' *Setter* rose under the persuasion of up-angled hydroplanes.

'Yes. It's them, all right. White flag, and a dark sweater. They're holding them out, two of them. No wind.'

Olsen felt like shouting with excitement and delight. Everyone was grinning with pleasure; except MacGregor, who had too much to think about, and Hutchins, who, with his eyes half closed, was too busy listening to the murmur and crackle in his headphones.

'Half ahead together. Port ten.'

'Port ten, Sir . . . Ten o' port wheel on, Sir.'

'Steer oh-six-oh. Special casing party, stand by!'

Olsen stepped forward. Hallet and Hughes moved up behind him: a Leading Torpedoman was on the fore 'planes, in Hallet's place. Each man carried a coiled heaving line slung over his shoulder, and both of them, and Olsen as well, wore their blue-covered lifebelts strapped across their chests.

MacGregor said, 'Open the lower gun-tower hatch. Olsen – your two men can get up on the ladder.'

'Aye aye, Sir.' The gun-tower ladder was already rigged in the wardroom, its top end clamped below the hatch and its foot screwed to the deck. The table had been unscrewed and dragged aside to make way for it. The lower hatch clanged open, and Hallet climbed up with Hughes behind him on the short ladder.

'Stand by to surface!'

MacGregor was still at the periscope, watching the boat

as *Setter* closed in towards it. Now he clicked the periscope into low power, and swept all round, quickly, checking the sky for aircraft. There weren't any, and he came back to watching the fishing boat. He said, 'They've seen the periscope. They're waving, and jumping about.' He smiled, now, watching them. Then the smile faded.

'What the hell's the matter with them? They've gone mad – or – Number One, bring her up to twenty-six feet.'

'Twenty-six feet, Sir . . . Ready to surface, Sir.'

MacGregor was talking half to himself. 'They're all pointing at something over . . . so *that*'s it!' He shoved up the handles of the periscope, and stepped back quickly. 'Forty feet! Group up, full ahead together! Olsen get those men out of the gun-tower. *Stand by gun action!*'

A rush of movement, muttered surprise as the gun's crew assembled rapidly in the wardroom. *Setter* was nosing down to forty feet, preparing for an explosive ascent into the light of day. MacGregor told the helmsman, 'Steer oh-four-oh.'

Olsen reported, 'Gun's crew closed up, Sir.'

'Good. Target an enemy launch. E-boat. Bearing, right ahead. Range three thousand yards, deflection twelve left. *Shoot.*'

Olsen shouted the orders up to the Gunlayer, who was up the ladder in the tower, with the gun's telescope slung round his neck and the Trainer close below him. The order *shoot* meant that the Layer could open fire as soon as his sights were on the enemy. Below the hatch, in the wardroom, the rest of the gun's crew waited, and behind them the two men whose job was ammunition supply had the first shells ready on the deck.

In the Control Room, the lower hatch was open. Mac-Gregor jumped on to the ladder.

'Surface!'

Olsen climbed up the ladder with his head overlapping the Captain's boots. *Setter*, at full speed now with her tanks blowing and the hydroplanes at hard a-rise, was shooting up like a cork. When the needles in the depth-gauges showed her depth to be fifteen feet, Crawshaw blew a long, loud blast on his whistle, and MacGregor flung the hatch open. Through a rain of salt water he and Olsen flung themselves up into the swimming bridge: *Setter* wasn't by any means right up, but the secret of successful gun actions was to get the first shot off before the enemy even knew you were there. Olsen scrambled up from the front of the bridge on to the sloping top of the cab, the front of the tower itself; his clothes were soaking wet. He grabbed the fixed torpedo sight for support and looked down on the heads of the gun's crew: almost in the same moment, the gun fired, an appalling noise for so small a weapon, particularly up here where he got the full blast of it in his ears. He thought, That gunlayer's *good*! He saw the enemy launch right ahead of them, the fishing boat thirty degrees off to port: he watched for the fall of the shell and saw it, in line but short. He yelled down to the sightsetter, 'Up four hundred – shoot!'

Immediately, the gun fired again: the launch was going flat out to reach the fishing boat, its bow high in the air on a mountain of white foam. But it wasn't an E-boat – more like an Air-Sea Rescue launch.

That shot was over, and slightly left. Olsen shouted to the gunlayer, 'Right six, down two hundred, shoot!' Behind him, MacGregor yelled into the voicepipe, 'Port ten. Steer oh-four-oh.'

A hit! Olsen almost screamed, 'No correction, *shoot*!' Then he realised that in the excitement of the lucky shot which had pinpointed the target so quickly, he'd made a mistake: the shell had burst on the enemy's stern in a sudden whoof of orange flame and black, spreading smoke, and the launch was all but stopped, her bow had fallen right back into the sea as she lost way and more flames, higher than the first, sprang out of the smoke which smothered her stern. The shot now on its way to her would miss, fall to the left, because there was a left deflection on the gunsight to allow for the enemy's previous speed.

'Right six, shoot!' The last shell fell left, as he'd expected. He waited for the next, and saw it go over, but only just, and right in line. 'Down one hundred, shoot!'

A machine gun of some light calibre was firing in short bursts from the launch's bow: *Setter*'s next shell burst on the waterline just below it, and the for'ard part of the launch disintegrated into flying debris and smoke and flame: the stern still floated, blazing. Olsen looked round at the Captain, asking a question without the need of words: MacGregor nodded, and Olsen yelled down to the gun's crew, 'Check, check, check! Secure the gun and go below. Good shooting!' Faces already grimed by cordite fumes grinned up at him as the Trainer swung the gun back fore-and-aft and the Loader clamped it. They were throwing the empty shell cases over the side, and the Layer was unshipping his telescope. Olsen slid down into the bridge, ripping his trousers on the projection of the torpedo sight and cursing with annoyance.

MacGregor had turned *Setter* towards the fishing boat. He called down the voicepipe, 'Group down, half ahead together.' Straightening, he nodded approval to Olsen. 'Nice work, Sub. Are the gun's crew out of the way, yet?'

Olsen checked. 'Yes, Sir.' MacGregor went back to the voicepipe. 'Hallet and Hughes on the casing, through the gun-tower hatch . . . You go down too, Olsen; starboard side-to.'

'Aye aye, Sir.' He climbed over the side of the bridge and down the fixed steel rungs to the catwalk which ran around its sides and linked the for'ard and after casings. Holding on to the brass rail, which was now greenish from salt water, he edged round on to the gun platform: Hallet was already there, sorting out the coils of his heaving line, and Hughes was just climbing out of the hatch. They stood in a group, feeling the heat from the breech and barrel of the gun, looking across the sea at the fishing boat and the people standing in her cockpit. Olsen realised that he'd had no time, up to now, to give it more than a glance: his attention had been fully occupied by the enemy launch and by the performance of the three-inch gun's crew. But now, looking hard at the sturdy *Redningsskøyte*, and recognising it immediately for what it was, he was sure that he could see five people and that three of them were women. Which, of course, was quite wrong . . .

MacGregor was facing the same puzzle. Examining the boat through his binoculars, he was quite certain of their numbers and of their sexes: two men, three women . . . Well, there'd been a switch in the rendezvous, so quite possibly there'd been a change in the party's composition, too. In any case, it didn't matter: the Petty Officer's mess had five bunks in it, and it could accommodate three women just as easily as two.

'Slow ahead starboard. Stop port.' He was heading clear of the boat's stern, intending to swing up to port and lay *Setter*'s starboard side alongside her.

'Port twenty. Stop starboard.' *Setter* began to swing, and MacGregor shouted down, 'Slow astern port.' The port motor went astern, swinging the submarine faster and at the same time taking the way off her.

'Midships. Starboard ten.' *Setter* was actually moving astern, now, swinging into position. 'Stop together. Midships.' Now just a touch ahead would put her neatly alongside. 'Slow ahead starboard.'

From the for'ard casing, Hallet tossed his heaving line in a graceful arc which sent the heavy knot flying across the bow. One of the two men ran for'ard and grabbed hold of it. A few moments later, the submarine and the fishing boat lay alongside each other, rocking to the swell, the planks of the smaller craft's hull creaking and straining as they jostled in the sea's movement.

Hallet and Hughes were down on the saddle-tanks: each man held on to apertures in the submarine's casing with one hand and stretched the other out to take hold of the Norwegians as they clambered gingerly over the low, wooded bulwark, and, in obvious trepidation, jumped the narrow gap. Olsen stayed on the casing, ready to take their hands and haul them up. He saw that another man would be needed, at the hatch: he yelled to the Captain, who was leaning over the front of the bridge, 'One extra hand, Sir, at the gun-tower hatch?' The Captain raised a hand in acknowledgement, and it was Ellis who came up, grinning all over his leathery face.

The first passenger was an elderly woman, almost certainly the bishop's wife. Trousers didn't suit her, and she was not built for acrobatics, for clambering from one moving ship to another. Olsen took charge of her from the men on the tanks, and lugged her up on to the casing.

'Fru Dalen?' She smiled, panting hard. 'Why, yes – and you – you're Norwegian?'

'Yes. If you would go to him –' he pointed at Ellis, by the hatch. 'As quickly as you can?'

'Of course. I *do* thank you –' He called after her. 'Be careful – mind your step!'

Then the two girls. Both beautiful! One fair, blue-eyed, with the lithe figure of a dancer: the other dark, brown-eyed, a bit more solid but perhaps, too, more attractive... As Olsen helped the yellow haired girl aboard, he asked her, 'You're Miss Dalen?'

'Yes! You're *Norwegian*! Oh, how *lovely*!' She threw her arms around his neck and kissed him warmly on the mouth. She said, looking as if she was going to burst into tears at any moment, 'Oh, but I'm so *happy*!'

Olsen disentangled himself, and pointed to Ellis, who was laughing his head off. 'Please – that way. Quickly.' He bent to help up the next girl, the dark one: but she was sure-footed and hardly needed assistance. She smiled and told him, 'I'm Anna. I know – I go *that* way.'

In a dream, Olsen greeted the bishop. 'Sir – I am so very honoured, I can't say . . . ' Looking into the tired, smiling eyes, he checked himself. 'Would you go that way, Sir, please? That sailor will show you . . . '

Last came Kjellegard, and Olsen, naturally enough, took him for a priest. It was a surprise, therefore, when the man seized his hand in a fist that could have throttled an ox, and shouted in his face, 'Glad to know you, lad. I'm Colonel Kjellegard. I'm a Gunner, and I'll tell you one thing – you fellows know how to shoot!'

.   .   .   .

When the passengers were all inside the submarine, Olsen sent the two seamen down after them and told Hallet to shut and clip the gun-tower hatch. Then he climbed up the side of the bridge, to report to the Captain.

'All aboard, Sir. Hatch shut.'

'Thank God for that.' *Setter* was going astern, clearing the fishing boat. MacGregor said into the voicepipe, 'Stop together. Starboard twenty. Half ahead together.' He turned to Olsen. 'I'm going to take a gander at what's left of that launch. There just might be a survivor . . . Midships! Steady as you go!'

Olsen picked up his binoculars: he'd left them in the bridge after the shooting was finished, because they'd have got in his way, down there on the casing. He focused them on the vague dotting of wreckage: there wasn't much, only bits and pieces, and still a greyish haze of smoke which hung above the sea where the launch had gone down. Some of the floating wood was still smoking.

'I don't think there will be a survivor, Sir.'

'Nor do I – but we'll make sure . . . Keep an all-round lookout, will you?' MacGregor turned aft, and spoke to the Oerlikon and Vickers gunners, who were looking fed-up because they'd had nothing to shoot at. 'All right, you three. Down you go.'

Olsen had swept all round, quickly. Now he started again, slowly and more carefully. MacGregor asked him, 'What the hell was all that necking, Olsen? Eh? You're a fast worker, aren't you?'

Olsen was glad that he was too busy to look at the Captain. 'It is just, I think, she was pleased to meet a Norwegian. She had not expected –'

' 'M.' MacGregor stooped to the voicepipe. 'Slow together.' He said to Olsen, 'There's nothing here that could possibly be alive.' Olsen looked over the side of the bridge: among the floating wood, the rubbish, he saw what MacGregor had meant. He looked away, quickly.

'No, Sir.'

'Well, that's that.' MacGregor looked at his watch. 'We'll stay up here for half an hour or so, just to get out a bit.' He shouted into the voicepipe, 'Steer two-seven-oh. Stop together. In both engine clutches.' He straightened, and told Olsen, 'You can stay up here while Soames gets himself a bite of grub. I'll send up the lookouts. When the engine clutches are in, stick on three-sixty revs. No – three-eighty. O.K.?'

'Aye aye, Sir.'

MacGregor dropped into the hatch while *Setter* swung, slowing, on to the westerly course. The voicepipe called, 'Bridge!'

'Bridge.'

'Both engine clutches in, Sir.'

'Half ahead together. Three-eight-oh revs.'

The diesels spluttered and roared into grumbling, pounding rhythm, and the submarine drove ahead, her bow pointing seawards, towards the deep water. Olsen lifted his binoculars and set himself to the routine of scanning the horizon, at the same time disliking the fact that he was stuck up here on the bridge when he might have been performing his liaison duties down below. Well, in half an hour they'd be dived, and he'd be off watch until ten thirty: breakfast, and bags of time for chatting to the Dalen family and to Anna whatever-her-name-was. He'd liked the look of Kjellegard, too: a solid, companionable sort of fellow. Presumably he'd been working in the Resistance, too: perhaps as the Bishop's bodyguard. Oh, there'd be plenty to hear!

He thought, Where the hell are those lookouts? He swung round, thinking that perhaps they'd come up already without reporting, and that in concentrating on his looking-out he hadn't heard them.

If he'd not turned, he wouldn't have seen the Messerschmidt . . .

It was streaking up astern, low to the sea, almost skimming the waves: he hadn't heard a thing and it was far too late to dive. If he dived the submarine now the 'plane would catch her as she started down, helpless, wallowing: the only thing he could do was take avoiding action, alter course sharply to throw the pilot off as he attacked – which meant *now* –

'Hard a-starboard!' His voice sounded in his own ears as a scream and he heard it repeated distantly in the voicepipe, but then that and all other sound was drowned in the stammer and crash of cannon-fire as the fighter swept over: it had soared like a swallow to swoop again across the submarine, cannons and machine-guns blazing: a hole appeared, jagged and hot in the smoking side of the bridge behind him, and the wooden coping flew up in a shower of splinters: a blow in the back threw him forward, steel talons tearing the flesh of his back and brilliant orange flashes in his eyes: he thought, frantically, *This can't be happening*, and he was in the corner of the bridge, slumped over the voicepipe: he tried to shout into it but all that came from his lips was blood, drips first and then a spurt as he strove to speak: no sound came, only blood spattering the copper rim, he wasn't at all sure what was happening or why. His back was burning, that was sure, he could feel the flames and, lower, a peculiar dullness in his legs: pain spread from his back into his chest as if the fire was boring through. Again he tried to shout and couldn't, couldn't even whisper: dropping to his knees with his head against the steel wall that was the side of the bridge he forced down on the bar which operated the cocks on the voicepipes, and he coughed blood all over his own hands as they gripped it and the pain rose in him with the effort, small as it was, normally a nothing; a single kick with one foot was all it needed at other times.

When it was shut he crawled around in a tight, painful circle, dragged himself to the hatch, somehow slid his legs into it: he had an impression, dream-like, of the 'plane banking overhead, high, arcing a wing against the cloud which drifted across blue sky and for some reason had no longer anything to do with him.

His feet couldn't grip on the ladder, couldn't even find a rung. He hung with his elbows and forearms jammed on the rim of the hatch coamings and he reached up quickly to grab the brass handle on the inside of the heavy lid: holding it, he slid into the void of the hatch and it clanged down hard with all his weight hanging from it by that one hand: he hung there in the sudden dark of the closed conning-tower while the pain screamed in his chest and back: he groped blindly, frantically, for the push-button of the klaxon and jabbed it twice with the thumb of his free hand. He heard the noise break out there below his dangling legs and sweat ran down his face, sweat or blood or both: his left hand found one of the clips under the hatch and dragged it shut. The noise of the sea rose like distant music, a roll of drums but soft, a background to the voices shouting up at him. He didn't hear the words in the voices, only the noise, which was nothing, tiny, to the roaring in his head. His hand, wet and slimy, began to slip on the smooth, round, brass: the arm applauded that, but the palm and fingers struggled to hold on: a hammer was at work in his brain, bringing back those orange flashes to explode in his face and eyes, and the flames swept up his back and licked around his ribs, clawed pincers working at his spine.

The hand opened, surrendering to the arm and to the multiple attacks of agony. Olsen fell a dozen feet, his body heavy, inert, dropping like a sack of rocks: it struck the rim of the lower hatch and went on down, knocking Mac-

Gregor, who'd been coming up to help him or to find out what he was doing, into a jarred, sprawling heap on the deck of the Control Room.

18

'I'LL stand his watches.' MacGregor stood beside the wardroom table, fiddling absently with the poker dice which lay on it in a pool of five around their leather cup. Crawshaw glanced up sharply.

'Oh no, Sir. Soames and I'll keep watch-and-watch. It's only a couple of days, won't hurt us.'

'I dare say it wouldn't. But I'm not making offers, or asking for argument, Number One. As I said, I'll stand Olsen's watches, as from midnight.'

'Aye aye, Sir.' Crawshaw thought, He's wrong. He reckons it's his fault that Olsen got shot up, and to salve his conscience he's making a whopping error. A commanding officer has to be ready to cope with emergencies, fit and fresh at any time of the day or night. Not half stupefied from lack of sleep, his judgment clouded and muzzy just when everything depends on his being right on the ball . . . Well, that's it. Pray God for a quiet passage home.

MacGregor stepped out into the gangway to let Bishop Dalen squeeze in past the table. The bishop had been shaving, in the wardroom W.C.; he carried his razor and a tube of shaving cream in his left hand, a towel slung over his shoulder. With his other hand, he touched his newly-smooth cheeks.

'So much better. To be unshaved, it makes a man feel tired. Dirty.' He chuckled. 'I am *still* dirty, but it doesn't feel so bad.' He held out the tube to MacGregor. 'Thank you, Captain.'

'Keep it, Sir, please. I've another.' He thought, I'll use Crawshaw's.

'Thank you, then.' The bishop put the gear, on top of the towel, in the drawer which had been emptied for his use. It held everything of his that had been in the pack he'd brought with him: mostly they'd been things of his wife's and daughter's.

It was mid-morning: *Setter* was at sixty feet, the electric motors driving her slowly out to sea. Soames was on watch in the Control Room; he and Crawshaw had decided to do three-hour stints instead of two, so that the man off-duty would have reasonable time for sleep. Once you were on watch, well, you were there, awake, and an extra hour didn't make all that much odds; but a two-hour break hardly allowed time for getting turned-in and then out again. But now, of course, with MacGregor putting himself on the roster, they'd be back to the normal routine of two hours on and four off.

Unless, thought Crawshaw, smiling to himself, a man forgot to shake the Captain . . . but, no. It wouldn't work, and there'd be hell to pay afterwards. Perhaps he'd be able to persuade the Captain to stand only night watches, or day ones . . .

The bishop sank on to the bench, and glanced with interest at the poker dice. He'd asked, during breakfast, a lot of questions as to how they spent their hours off-duty. The answer had been in the main, 'We sleep!' But when someone had mentioned the game of Liar Dice, the bishop had said he'd like to learn it. This was the hour appointed for the lesson. He looked up, smiling, as MacGregor pulled back the chair and sat down facing him across the table: but looking at MacGregor's face, the bishop's smile faded.

'You are blaming yourself for –' he jerked his head, to point for'ard. They'd got Olsen in one of the lower bunks in the Ladies' Boudoir: the women had insisted on it, and it was quite certainly the best place for him. The *only* place. Here in the wardroom it would be disturbed with noise and movement: but in the women's space there'd be no one going up on watch, or coming back to sleep: less noise, too, from the diesels and from the routine working of the Control Room. They'd all of them have their meals in the wardroom, and the women would take watches of their own, as nurse. At this moment, Anna was sitting beside his bunk, continually bathing his head and face and hands with cool, damp cloths, watching the rate of his pulse.

But he wasn't going to live.

.   .   .   .

They'd doctored him first (if it could be called doctoring) on the deck of the Control Room, where he'd fallen. Not the women: they'd been kept out of it, and the Cox'n had gone to work with the textbook open beside him and Kjellegard as his assistant. Kjellegard knew about as much as the Cox'n did, on the subject of First Aid and emergency treatments: their combined knowledge didn't add up to much and there hadn't been time to read all the chapters in the book. But then, lacking a hospital, there wasn't much that could be done in any case. They'd straightened him out and got the clothes off him (Able Seaman Sellers had fainted at the sight of the lacerated, punctured back) and they'd washed out the wounds so far as they could, with antiseptic swabs. Then they'd put pads over the wounds and bound them tight with yards of bandage

183

all around his chest, strained them so tight that it would have hurt if Olsen had been conscious – which he wasn't – but they had to stop the bleeding and that was the only way to do it. What he needed was a blood transfusion, according to the book and common sense: but there was no equipment for that. The bindings didn't stop the flow of blood; it seeped through the pads and stained the bandages but there was nothing else to do, only hope that the dressing would slow the flow and eventually stop it . . .

They got him on a stretcher and carried him into the women's mess: as they were moving him, as gently as they could, face downwards on to the bunk, laying him on a spread blanket, he showed signs of coming-to: his hands began to clench and unclench and his breath came hard in a sound that was half a moan, half growl: there was no movement except for the convulsively jerking fingers, and his eyes stayed shut, the lids a blueish colour on his pale, drained face. They covered him up to his neck with another blanket, giving him no pillow because the Cox'n reckoned he'd be better kept flat. Kjellegard bent Olsen's arms at the elbows, so that his hands lay above the top edge of the blanket, on either side of his face; the arms were limp, unresisting, but the hands still clenched and straightened like the parts of some machine that wouldn't stop, and breath hissed roughly in his throat, a noise like sandpaper moving against itself.

The Cox'n had sterilised a syringe and filled it with morphine, according to the book's instructions, but they hadn't wanted to give it to him when he'd seemed to be already unconscious: but now, from the movement of his hands and the erratic, choking breath, it seemed that it was more likely some degree of paralysis than total unconsciousness. Kjellegard pulled back the top of the blanket to bare an arm and a shoulder and, looking up at the Cox'n, he nodded his head at the syringe. The Cox'n took it, swabbed the arm with ether: he bent forward, poising the needle, but his hand was trembling and sweat began to run down his suddenly greenish face. Kjellegard took the syringe out of the Cox'n's hand, and gave Olsen the inject-ion. Withdrawing the needle, he asked the Cox'n, quietly, 'How much was this? A grain?'

The Cox'n shook his head. 'Half.' He pointed at the open textbook. 'It says there, that's normal, like.'

Kjellegard shook his head, and handed back the empty syringe. 'Another half grain.' The Cox'n hesitated, half turn-ing to go to his medical locker for another phial, then pausing, undecided. The Norwegian told him, gruffly, 'It is right, for this. I know morphine, from before. Often. Quickly, please.'

The Cox'n went for it, and Kjellegard rose to his feet. He and MacGregor were alone in the tiny mess, looking down on the blanketed figure on the bunk, at the grey-white face and the hands which still jerked open and shut, open and shut. Kjellegard put his mouth close to the Captain's ear and whispered. 'The boy's spine – it was shot, all broken. We can only keep him out of pain.'

.   .   .   .

'Number One. Go and find Chief, will you? Tell him and Colonel Kjellegard that we're all set for a Liars lesson.' Crawshaw nodded, and went aft. Chief was showing Kjellegard round the boat, explaining the purpose of every little pipe and valve. No doubt the Norwegian would be grateful to be rescued: it was extraordinary how engin-eers expected their own enthusiasm for things mechanical to be shared by normal people. Probably, when Kjellegard had asked to be shown through the submarine, he'd been thinking of a brisk stroll through the compartments, a glance at the periscope, another at the torpedo tubes. Instead of that, poor fellow, he'd be getting a lecture on the internal mechanism of the ballast pump, a discourse on hydraulics, some details of the tensile strength of welding as opposed to rivets. The only thing to be said for it was that he'd probably never ask another question, not while he was aboard *Setter*.

With Crawshaw gone, MacGregor answered the bishop's last assertion. He'd been wanting to.

'Yes, I do – blame myself. It was nobody's fault except mine; least of all Olsen's. I should have dived, to start with, not stayed on the surface. And staying up there, even if that had been right – which it wasn't – I shouldn't have left him on his own until the lookouts were up there too.'

Dalen scrubbed the tips of his fingers. He murmured, 'I should have scrubbed my fingernails. You have a brush I can lend?'

'Borrow. Yes. Now?'

'Oh, no. The next time, thank you . . . Tell me. You did not dive, then, for some *reason*. Eh?'

'Yes. I wanted to get out, offshore, a few miles, rather than dive where they'd know to start a search. Your boat was there, you see, to mark the spot. And we go faster on the surface than we can under water, you see.'

'Yes . . . So when you say that you should better have dived, that is not true. Please excuse me, Captain – I am trying to have it clear . . . You say, now, you should not leave him alone. If you had waited with him, the aeroplane would have still come – eh? You would have seen this in time, better than the boy did?'

MacGregor nodded, slowly. 'One of us would. Almost certainly.'

'Ah – *almost*. You are not sure. Now you say, the look-outs. If they had been going up there to him, immediately when you came down from there: I think they could be getting there at the same time as the aeroplane arrive, that moment? Then three men, not one, would perhaps be shot?'

'It's possible. But –'

The bishop raised a finger. 'So. And if young Olsen was looking about him as he should, would he not have seen this machine?'

'Perhaps, Sir. We don't know where it came from. Out of a cloud: but there wasn't much. There might have been a patch of mist – I don't remember. One man alone can't look in every direction at once . . . It was my carelessness, Bishop. Mine. *I'm* responsible for – for the fact that Olsen's dying.'

The bishop picked up one of the dice and turned it slowly in his fingers, examining the six faces one after the other. 'These are faded. You play a lot, this game . . . Captain – if you determine for yourself you are responsible – for blame – the *carelessness*, you say . . . then there is not logic, not point to argue. It is your wish to have it so. And I could say to you, "I, Dalen, I have made men fight the Germans in Norway, I have told them they are right to do this, that our enemy is evil and we should play our part in so small way as we can, to his defeat." I have told them, God is with us: I have asked His blessing for their work.'

The bishop looked up suddenly, and his eyes held Mac-Gregor's almost in a challenge. 'So many die. Many. In their fighting and as hostage. Women, too, as hostage. They say, "Stop – or we kill these people you love." Norwegian people ask me, *me*, "What shall we do?" I have said to them, "*Fight*. Do not allow this weapon to the devil. We do not fight for you, or you, or you. Not for your wife, your mother. We fight for Norway, for the world, for God." So people are killed, from what I have said. Innocent people, young, old – *people*. This, for what I have been saying when the people ask, "What shall we do, Bishop Dalen?" So, Captain, I have killed these men, women. *I* am responsible. I have done it for nothing that you can see today: in Norway, still they are murdering our people. But *I*, Captain, *I* – and I am a priest. But am I still a man of God? Captain, I tell you, *I don't know.*'

The bishop looked down at his hands as they knotted into fists: surprisingly large, powerful fists, the backs of them covered with gingery hair.

'Captain, if I permitted myself to think as you are thinking now, then I could cut my throat!'

Kjellegard coughed. He said, 'This, Sir, is no proper speech for bishops.' He turned, throwing an arm round the engineer's shoulders. 'This man here, Sir, has revealed to me all his secrets. There are pipes for air, pipes for water, pipes for oil. All are different colours painted, so you do not mix them up. On every pipe there is nine hundred little wheels; then there is wiring, cables, forty thousand miles of these, and on each wire is seven hundred switches, all painted red and blue and green. All this I know. But one thing remains to me a problem, and I must ask it now before we play your game, or, dear Bishop Dalen, if you will excuse me saying it, I will surely burst: I went in there, but there is no chain, and I did not like –'

MacGregor jumped up. 'I'm *so* sorry!' He thought, The women, too! No one's showed them! Well, this is mechanics. 'Chief –'

The engineer nodded. It was in his own interests that the visitors should be able to manage that equipment properly:

when it was used by the unskilled, the whole thing jammed and flooded, and it was Featherstone's job to put it right again. It took the E.R.A. off other work, and it made him angry for days after the event, and this upset the smooth running of Chief's department.

He got right inside the little closet, and the two Norwegians, neither of them small men, crowded each other in the open doorway and stared without confidence at the gauges and curling pipes which lined the inside of the hull. Chief said, 'Now. Imagine you've done it.'

Kjellegard smiled wistfully. 'I wish I could. But it is not so easy.' The bishop chuckled.

'Well. *There –*' Chief balled a piece of Admiralty-issue paper, and dropped it in the pan. 'That's it. Now the principle is, it's got to be dropped down into a lower chamber – like into the breech of a gun, sort of – and then blown out into the sea.' He put his hand on the cylinder in the corner. 'This is the air vessel. First, we have to build up the right pressure in it. Like this.' He opened a small valve, and they saw the needle begin to move in the gauge above the cylinder. When it reached a painted mark, Chief shut the valve. 'So far, so good. All right?' They both nodded, two overgrown schoolboys being introduced to algebra. 'Now,' continued Chief, warming to his task, 'we take hold of this lever, push the latch off it, and pull it to *this* position. You see now, the trap's opened, but the whatnot hasn't dropped. Right – open this valve here, and in shoots the water. See?'

Again they nodded, watching closely as he turned the water off. 'Now, it's most important to check that this big hull valve, this chap down, here, is open. If you don't, and it's shut, you'll be in a bit of a mess very soon afterwards. Don't *ever* forget to see that it's open – *please.*' Chief straightened slightly, moving cautiously so as not to bang his head. 'Now we're ready to fire. First, open this valve here, then – if you're sure you've done all those other things, mind – you open *this* one, and – *whoosh!*' There was a loud hiss, and a gurgling sound below the trap in the pan. He looked round at them, and smiled. 'That bit of paper is now drifting up toward the surface. Quite easy, isn't it?'

Neither of them commented. Chief pointed at the pan. 'Colonel, perhaps you'd like to do it now?' Chief pressed himself back against the bulkhead, to give Kjellegard room for manoeuvre.

Kjellegard's eyebrows rose. 'You are going to watch?' The bishop guffawed, and banged his head on an overhead valve; he stopped laughing immediately, and muttered a short word in his own language. Kjellegard glanced at him in sharp surprise, and the bishop muttered, again in Norwegian, what sounded like an apology. Chief said, 'Just a practice shot, Colonel. Like I've just done . . . Here.' He dropped in another ball of paper.

MacGregor had been standing in the gangway behind them, listening to the lecture. He stuck his head forward over the bishop's shoulder and reminded the engineer, 'There's Olsen's instructions in the box, Chief. They can use that to check with, each time.' He went on past them, and tapped on the outside of the Ladies' Boudoir. Anna's face appeared in a gap in the curtains. MacGregor asked her, 'How is he?'

She whispered, 'The same, Captain. He does not move. But his breath is better, I think. Come in –'

MacGregor hesitated. 'Are the others –?'

'Yes, come in, Captain.' Anna smiled. 'They are still sleeping in their beds. Very tired, I think, and your so good breakfast making us sleepy also.'

MacGregor stepped cautiously into the little, screened-off space. Curtains were drawn over two of the bunks on the other side, but on this lower bunk, where Olsen lay, they were looped up over the rail. Olsen's face was deadly pale against the greyish-yellow blanket: but he was still now, his hands limp, and the breath hissed evenly between his clenched teeth. Anna dipped her cloth in the can of water on the table, and wrung it out; as MacGregor stepped back, she leant down and smoothed it gently across the white, glistening forehead.

MacGregor asked her, whispering, 'Is there anything you need?'

She shook her head, smiling, but not looking up. 'Thank you. You are very kind to us.'

.　　.　　.　　.　　.　　.　　.　　.　　.

'Now then.' MacGregor smothered a yawn. 'We'll teach you this game.' Crawshaw was back, now, so there were five of them close together around the table. He thought, Those women have got some sense! Here we are, playing ruddy dice in the middle of the forenoon when we ought to be catching up on sleep – and all out of politeness to these blokes who'd almost certainly rather be dossing down themselves and are only trying to keep awake out of politeness to *us*. How the hell did it start? He thought, After lunch, there'll be no games, no talking. Just *sleep*! He picked up the dice, and asked the bishop, 'Do you know the hands of poker, Sir? Ordinary poker, with cards?'

The bishop shook his head. 'But I have always wished to know this, Captain. You will explain?'

Oh, my God! To teach a foreign bishop poker – and Liars at that – from scratch! Well – here goes . . .

'Each dice has six faces, and each face is a card. The

lowest is a nine – see? – then ten, jack, queen, king, ace. Now, the best hand anyone can have is five aces – that's quite plain, Sir, isn't it? Well, then, now I'll give you the order of the hands . . . '

Presently, they were making practice throws, and the bishop seemed to have the hang of it that far; Kjellegard needed no instruction. MacGregor drew a deep breath. 'Now,' he said. 'Liars.' He thought, This is going to be the hard part . . .

'In Liars, we tell lies. Hence the name. You throw your hand of dice, but you throw it hidden, and you don't let anyone else see it. But you have to say what it is – that is what it probably *isn't* – when you pass it on to the next man. Then if he doesn't believe you, he says "lift it". You have to expose the hand, and if you've lied, you lose a life. But if what you've said is there *is* there, then *he's* lost. You see?'

'No.' The bishop shook his head. 'I am sorry, Captain, I do not understand. *Why* must I lie?'

MacGregor scratched his head. 'It's always difficult to explain, at first, this game. But – well, let me put it this way. Suppose you've made the first throw, and you say it's three tens, and I take it, then whatever it is I'm stuck with it and and I've got to pass on something higher. But if, on –'

They looked up, to see why he'd suddenly stopped talking. There was a tense expression in his face, and he seemed to be listening: Chief opened his mouth to say something but the Captain raised a hand to check him. 'Wait –'

They heard Soames's voice, from the Control Room. 'Are you *sure* it's H.E.?' The Asdic operator of the watch, a man named Rogers who came from Liverpool, sounded as if he was surprised that his report should have been queried. 'Yessir – *H.E.* - Green one-oh. Reciprocating.'

MacGregor was out of the wardroom in a flying leap in

the same moment that Soames called, urgently, 'Captain, Sir!' Muttering 'Excuse me', Crawshaw squeezed out behind Kjellegard and followed more slowly into the Control Room. The Asdic operator spoke again: 'Second H.E., Sir. Red two-four. It's increasing, Sir.' His voice rose. 'Transmissions on both bearings, Sir.'

'Stop port.' MacGregor glanced at the depth-gauges: *Setter* was at exactly sixty feet. 'Number One – take over the trim, please. One hundred feet.' He crossed over to the Asdic corner, and jammed the spare headset over his ears: he listened for a few seconds, and then took it off. In a tone of disgust, he muttered 'Same pair as last time . . . same class, anyway. Soames – go through all compartments, and tell everyone to keep still and quiet. No talk, no movement. Quick, now.'

'Aye aye, Sir.' Soames didn't take long over it: hardly anyone was awake, apart from the watchkeeper. He left the wardroom to the last, stopping there on his way back. He told the two Norwegians, 'There are hunting craft above us. It's essential we make no noise, and the Captain asks that you should not talk or move about.'

Kjellegard whispered, 'Hunting? For us?' Soames smiled and nodded. 'Nothing to worry about. This often happens.' He went on, into the Control Room, and what he'd said to the Norwegians reminded him, briefly, of his own first patrol. It had been in the Mediterranean, from Malta: they'd had over a hundred charges dropped on them and the destroyers kept them down for a day and a half. Some of the battery containers were cracked, and a propeller shaft was bent so that they had only one engine they could use for the limp back to Malta. The air had gone foul, too, during the long spell under water, and they'd had trays of chemical laid out to absorb the poison of the

Carbon Dioxide . . . But it had been his first patrol, and since nobody in the boat had shown any sign of fear or even worry, he'd assumed that it was fairly normal procedure and hadn't been too frightened himself.

Now it was like that for the passengers. Whatever was about to happen, it was imperative that they should think it was routine, a matter of no moment, no cause for worry . . .

He nodded to MacGregor, indicating that he'd done what he'd been told. At the same moment the Asdic operator reported, 'Enemy Red two-one in contact, Sir.' MacGregor swore, quietly.

'Soames. Get all the passengers into the P.O.'s mess, all together. *Quickly.*' The Captain paused, giving the Norwegians time to move before the rush started. Then: 'Half ahead together. Starboard twenty. Diving Stations: Shut off for depth-charging!'

Chief was on his way through to the engine room. MacGregor stopped him. 'Chief. I want you in the After Ends, please. Same orders as last time.' He thought, *This is where we came in . . .*

.   .   .   .

19

KJELLEGARD started, and looked up at the white-painted deckhead. The bishop glanced up too, and Kari asked them, 'What was it – that noise?'

Dalen shrugged. 'Who knows? I don't even know how this craft works, what makes it go up or down. It's all a mystery, to me.'

Kjellegard nodded. 'It made me jump, whatever it was. Nerves! I've not got over the sight of that launch coming out after us. That thing, and no sign of the submarine -- I don't mind admitting it, I hadn't much hope left, just then. If they'd got to us first, these people wouldn't have been able to do anything. They wouldn't have been able to shoot without hitting us too.' He shook his head, as if it still worried him, even as a memory. 'They'd have had it all their own way!'

'But –' the bishop was frowning – 'surely, the Germans would have shot us, there and then. Eh?'

Kjellegard shook his head. 'No. The rest of us, perhaps, but not you, Sir. They wanted you alive. Those were their orders – we knew all about that.'

'Then what? Why me alive?'

Depth-charges exploded like thunder all around the submarine: she shuddered, and they felt a swing to port, a slight angling of the deck. The Norwegians looked at each other: none of them spoke. Anna was bending over Olsen, and she didn't turn round. The echoes of the explosions died away, and Kjellegard cleared his throat.

'I expect that's the worst of it. These chaps know what they're doing – we're in good hands.'

A tall seaman stuck his head around the curtain. 'All right, ladies and gents? Nobody broke their specs?'

'Thank you, we are quite all right.' The bishop asked him, 'What was that?'

'Depth-charges, Sir. Don't worry – they can't do us no 'arm. There'll be a few more, though, I reckon.'

'Oh.' Mrs Dalen squeezed her husband's hand under the table. 'Is it always so noisy?'

'Noisy, ma'am? Why, that lot weren't *loud*. Y'see, it's always that quiet, like, down 'ere, they sound worse 'n what they really are.' The man chuckled, shaking his head. 'You don't want to let it disturb you . . . Well, I'm just along 'ere, if you should want me. Just sing out, like, and I'll be 'ere . . . Right, sir?'

The bishop smiled at him. 'Thank you. What is your name?'

'Meakin, Sir. Charlie Meakin.' The man withdrew, and Mrs Dalen said, 'What a nice sailor. But they don't *dress* like sailors, do they? I thought they had trousers with wide bottoms and shirts with little stripes along the top, and those flat caps.'

'And pigtails?' The bishop laughed, and patted her knee. 'I think they are allowed to dress as they like, in these submarines.' He turned to Kjellegard, ignoring the sound of a second lot of screws which churned the water overhead, growing louder to crescendo pitch then fading again to silence. Kjellegard was thinking, The last time we heard that, the explosions came after. The bishop asked him, 'Now what is this, that the Germans wanted to capture me alive? What for?'

'Partly as hostage, Sir. You in the hands of the Gestapo – it would have been more use to them than a thousand other hostages. All over Norway, people would have stopped fighting.'

'I hope they would not.' *Setter* trembled as her motors speeded. Dalen asked Kjellegard, 'You say *partly*. What's the rest of it?'

Explosions rocked the submarine: the deck angled steeply, as if she was diving: two more charges burst, the impact clanging on the hull, shaking her violently. Cork rained down: Kari picked up a chip of it, and looked at it closely.

'What's this stuff? It's fallen everywhere –'

'Cork, Miss.' Meakin was there, in the gap in the curtains. 'It's in the paint, like. Look –' Reaching up, he scraped a bit off the deckhead with his thumb-nail. 'See? Special paint, it is, for submarines. But it never stops falling off and we're always 'aving to sweep it up. Wouldn't like it in your 'ouse, I don't suppose, would you?'

Mrs Dalen laughed nervously. 'Another thing for sweeping up! Oh, no!'

'I bet you wouldn't, ma'am.' The sailor looked round at them all. ' 'Ow about a game, now? Got a pack o' cards? It'd 'elp to pass the time, like. Tell y' what – 'ow about Uckers?'

'Uckers?' Kjellegard shook his head. 'This is a game of dice, perhaps?'

Meakin nodded. 'Sort of. Look – 'ang on, and I'll fetch a set out of the Killicks' mess . . . '

'Oh, dear.' The bishop frowned at Kjellegard. 'If this is anything like the game they were trying to teach us along there – well, I don't want to learn it, it's gibberish. Now – Kjellegard – you were saying?'

'Oh. Yes, they wanted you alive, in order to discredit you to the nation. They would have said – "Here, here's your Bishop Dalen, the great man who means so much to you and who tells *you* to fight us: we've caught him slinking off to England – running away!" Think, Sir, what a weapon they'd make of that!'

'Yes.' Dalen spoke unhappily. 'And it'd be true.'

'No, it would not. You're leaving first because it's best for Norway that you should live, and second because you will continue your work from London. If you will forgive my putting it in a nutshell, Sir, this is a military operation and a political necessity, and you are obeying orders.'

'Obeying –!'

'Yes, Sir.' Their eyes met, the bishop's at first angry, Kjellegard's level and emotionless. Then Dalen smiled.

'Have it your way, then, Colonel – *Sir*.' They were all laughing when the sailor came back with the Uckers board and a little box containing dice and coloured counters. He put it down on the table, and opened the board.

'Why – it's *Ludo*! Mrs Dalen put a hand on her daughter's arm. 'Kari – Ludo! And he calls it – what is your word?'

'Uckers, Ma'am. Ludo – same thing. Only I reckon we 'ave different rules from what you do.' Meakin's eyes flickered as he heard the screws pass overhead. 'But if you know it, then play it your way, like. It's all 'ere – red, green, blue, yeller, Two dice. O.K., Sir?'

'O.K.' The bishop looked up at him. 'And we do thank you very much. I am afraid we are a nuisance, taking your time, your –' he waved a hand around – 'your space.'

'Not a bit of it, Sir. We're glad to 'ave you.' He went, and Mrs Dalen began to sort out the counters. The others watched her, waiting for the explosions.

Kari said, 'I don't think I want to play.' She swivelled round to Anna, perched on the edge of Olsen's bunk. 'Anna – you'll play? I'll take your place there.'

Anna whispered, 'No. I'll stay here. Please, I'd rather, truly.' The charges seemed to burst under their feet: the deck moved, and *Setter* jolted, lurched upwards: she swung listing hard to starboard while a final, solitary explosion crashed out astern. Cork chips littered the Ludo board.

Mrs Dalen brushed them off, and rearranged the counters: she'd had them in neat piles, according to colour, and the attack had sent them all over the table.

.   .   .   .

In the Tube Space, Chief Petty Officer Rawlinson sat on a wooden seat which was shaped rather like the saddle of a motor-bike. It was up between the tubes themselves, and pivoted, so that the T.I. could sit there and still reach the controls and the firing gear of all six tubes. He wore headphones which connected him directly with the Control Room. Behind him, on the wide step which ran behind the rear doors of the torpedo tubes, sat Able Seamen Hughes and Murchison. None of the three men had spoken during the last half hour. The compartment, over its deep, red-leaded bilges, smelt dankly of salt water.

A voice crackled in the T.I.'s telephone. 'Tube Space!' He answered, 'Tube Space', and the voice said, quickly, 'Stand by one, two, three and four tubes!'

The T.I. jerked upright in his seat. He repeated the order loudly, both as acknowledgement to the man in the Control Room and as an order to his two assistants. To them he added, 'One and two's already blown up. Blow up three and four. Lively, now!'

Valves were opened, high-pressure air sent thudding into the Water-Round-Tubes tank to blow water up through pipes into the tubes where it would surround torpedoes which, up to now, had been dry.

'Three blown up, T.I.'

'Four blown up.'

Rawlinson's hand moved to the levers which controlled the bow-caps, the heavy doors on the front ends of the tubes. Here inside the Tube Space, pointers moved slowly round on large brass discs, showing that those front covers on the top four tubes were swinging open to the sea.

'One, two, three and four bow-caps open, T.I.' Now, if some fish out there was looking at the submarine from right ahead of her bow, it would see the open ends of the tubes, and, inside them, the warheads of the torpedoes.

The T.I.'s hands moved to the group of firing levers, and pulled out four of the safety pins: then his big hands rested, just above the top two triggers. He said into his telephone, 'Control Room: One, two, three and four tubes ready.' He heard the man at the other end repeat his words to the Captain, and, very faintly, he could hear other orders: short, clipped words and sentences spoken in the Control Room which was shut off from here not only by distance but also by three lots of clamped, watertight doors. The T.I. thought, Mac's going to have a crack at one of them sods. Bloody good luck to him! He kept his eyes fixed on the firing levers under his hands, and waited for the order, which, every time it was given, marked a culmination of months of work.

He knew these four torpedoes pretty well: they'd been reloads, in the racks in the Fore Ends, throughout two patrols and the spells in harbour, and he'd done plenty of maintenance routines on them, checking their motors and igniters, topping up their air bottles and shale-oil fuel, fitting new detonators: routines he knew by heart, sequences of checks which he'd done, or supervised, for years on end on countless torpedoes: but still he never did it by memory, always by the book, checking each item before going on to the next. A few seconds' careless work or a glance the other way while someone else skimped the job could mean a fish would run off its course, or even not run at all . . .

'Stand by!'

'Stand by.' His fingers tensed, and he lowered his hands an inch, to touch the cold metal of the firing levers.

'Fire One!' Repeating the order, he pulled back on the first lever, heard the thud of compressed air as it banged into the rear end of the tube, felt the submarine tremble as the great, steel fish leapt and sped away towards an unseen enemy.

'Fire Two!' The hiss of venting air shrieked in their ears, a deafening noise in the cramped, rounded space. 'Fire Three!' That lever with his left hand: now the right waited on number four.

'Fire *Four*!' Again the jarring thud, the tremor of the ship: Chief Petty Officer Rawlinson grinned faintly to himself, and dropped his hands into his lap. He muttered, 'God bless 'em!' and his hands moved again, knowing their job, moving as if by instinct to the levers to shut the bow-caps on the four empty tubes. Into the mouthpiece of his telephone set he reported quietly, 'One, two, three and four tubes fired.' He felt the sudden dip of the bow and he thought, piecing things together in his mind, We're going deep, then. At the same time, he felt the vibration of suddenly increased speed. He'd no idea how many of the enemy there were up top: there might be another coming in, at this moment, to shower them with another batch of charges. Silence or bedlam: he was ready for either.

From behind and below him, Murchison asked, 'Ain't it time they 'it, T.I.?' Rawlinson grunted angrily: this waiting period was bad enough without stupid questions. 'When they do, me lad, you'll 'ear it. Till then keep your mouth shut, will you?'

There was no way of telling how long it would take the torpedoes to reach their target. It depended on the range: the fish travelled at forty knots, and the closer the enemy was, the sooner they'd reach him – hit, or pass. Couldn't be much of a target, or Mac would have fired a full salvo of six, instead of only four: but then, it might be that he simply didn't want *Setter* to have no torpedoes left, in case she ran up against something new on the way back. She had three, now: two in numbers five and six, here, and the one stern tube in her tail.

Rawlinson visualised the four torpedoes speeding towards the enemy. Echeloned and slightly fanned, he saw them running steadily, a team in which each unit kept station on the others, their gyros and servomotors holding them firmly to course and depth, a stream of bubbles rising to the surface fifty feet behind each of the racing screws . . .

The explosion was quite different to the noise a depth-charge made. For one thing, it was a long way off: for another, it was a sound as joyous as a peal of bells. Murchison gave a loud yell of excitement, and the T.I., who was still listening, snarled at him to be quiet: but when, just as he grated the words, 'Shut it, will yer!' they heard a second explosion exactly like the first, even Rawlinson lost his sense of decorum. He threw back his head, and laughed, and the two men behind him, shouting with delight, reached up to pound him on the back.

They were *his* fish that had done it . . .

. . . .

As soon as he'd fired the salvo, MacGregor took *Setter* down to a hundred and fifty feet: but he held the same course, following in the tracks of the torpedoes, or rather, under them, towards the enemy, with the submarine's motors going full ahead and grouped-up; his object was to keep the enemy's ears full of *Setter*'s own noise and thus smother the sound of the running torpedoes. The enemy he'd fired at had been stopped: they'd been using the same tactics – effective, but dangerous to themselves – as they had last time: and while the torpedoes were running the second ship had been coming in for another run over the top. But when the salvo struck, they broke off the attack, and from Hutchins's reports it was at once obvious that the undamaged ship had altered course to go to his partner's assistance.

Not that there'd be much left of that one. To have scored two hits on so small a ship was astounding, and totally unexpected. MacGregor had spaced his shots at the enemy and just ahead of him, to allow for his starting to move again while the salvo was on its way. Probably it was the first two which had done it: the one aimed right amidships, the other just on the bow. By now, that little ship which had been so uncannily accurate with its depth-charges would be well and truly sunk, and the other, no doubt, racing in to pick up survivors.

MacGregor forced the smile off his face. It wasn't easy, because everyone in the Control Room was grinning at him. He said, 'Starboard twenty. Sixty feet. Slow ahead together. Steer two-six-oh.' Coming back on to a westerly course left the remaining enemy away out on the submarine's port quarter: in any case, that fellow had his hands full, he'd be unlikely to bother them again.

Hutchins reported, happily, 'Breaking-up noises, Sir, Red one-six-oh.' MacGregor nodded, and asked him, 'Where's the other bloke?'

'Red one-three-two, Sir. Slowing.'

MacGregor thought, It's safe enough . . . I'll have a look. He told Crawshaw, 'Thirty-two feet, Number One.'

'Thirty-two feet, Sir.' He'd been busy settling the trim at sixty feet: now he had to start all over again, putting more water into the internal ballast as she rose towards the surface.

The needles passed forty feet, and MacGregor nodded to

Featherstone. 'Up periscope.' The E.R.A. eased up the long, steel lever: the periscope rose a foot, then slowed, inched upwards, stopped. Featherstone swore, in a whisper: he pushed the lever down, and the great, brass tube sank again to its housed position. He jerked the lever up hard: the periscope shot up fast, but stuck again in the same position.

'It's jammed, Sir.'

'Try the other.' MacGregor moved across to the after periscope, the low-powered, smaller one. It rose quickly, the greased wires hissing over the sheaves on the deckhead. Thirty-four feet: daylight danced in the Captain's eyes as he spun round quickly, checking for aircraft or anything close. Then, twisting more slowly on a second circuit, he muttered, 'I suppose that bloody aircraft hit the for'ard standard with a cannon shell. We'll see when we surface.'

He'd swept all round, and seen nothing. Now he swung the periscope round to look out over the port quarter, and he asked Hutchins, 'H.E. bearing now?'

'Red one-five-eight, Sir. Very faint – stopping, Sir.'

Stopping – no doubt to haul survivors out of the water. 'Twenty-eight feet, Number One.'

'Twenty-eight feet, Sir.'

Setter rose higher, almost nudging the surface. MacGregor stared hard into the periscope: then he grunted. 'Mast, and a bit of superstructure. That's all I can see . . . Down periscope.' He stepped back, rubbing his chin. 'Thirty-two feet.' He was tempted to relax, open up the water-tight doors, fall out from action stations. But that could be premature: better make sure. 'Hutchins. I want to know when that bugger moves, and which way. Watch him.'

'Aye aye, Sir.'

MacGregor thought, They take risks, these Germans. To stop, now, for survivors: in fact, he's safe to do it, but if I was a German I'd be using my last two fish on *him*, and the hell with men in the water. They did that in the first war, and they've done it since. It's his good fortune that we have scruples which his own people do without . . .

For ten minutes, nothing happened. *Setter* purred steadily out towards the west: in the warm, sealed compartments even a cough was a loud noise, and the ticking of the electric log was a small drumbeat in the silence. Then Hutchins said, 'Faint H.E. on bearing, Sir. *Going away.*'

MacGregor grinned. It had been worth waiting for! He said, 'Open up from depth-charging . . . Number One – which watch?'

Crawshaw consulted the Cox'n. 'White watch, Sir.'

'White watch – Watch Diving.'

While the watertight doors were being unclamped and opened, and while the men were changing round, swapping cheerful comments on this latest success, MacGregor leant against the ladder in the middle of the Control Room, weighing the facts in his mind, assessing the sum of the results. There wasn't a doubt, the Germans had taken more than a bloody nose: a U-boat, the Dalen party, and now an A/S trawler. (He wondered, briefly, if in the Patrol Report he could refer to it as a frigate. Well, Intelligence would soon give it a name; and in German, it would be twenty-six letters long.)

There'd been some unpleasant moments, and *Setter* had her scars to show for them. The shaft bearing that leaked, and now this jammed periscope: although that might not be as serious as it seemed. The top of the standard might have been bent, or gashed and a ribbon of metal forced over to stop the periscope rising. If that was all, they could fix it this evening, when they surfaced: a hacksaw, or an acetylene torch would clear it. So long as the periscope itself wasn't damaged: that was a job for highly skilled specialists on the Base staff. Well, with any luck, it wouldn't matter now, in any case: *Setter* would surface tonight, and she wouldn't have to dive again. Forty-eight hours on the surface, and they'd be in Lerwick. No doubt the passengers would be taken from them there, and flown down to London. *Setter* would go on back to her flotilla, at Dundee: to repair the damage, ten days' leave to half the ship's company, fill up with stores and torpedoes and then off again for another patrol. Perhaps, this time, a quiet one . . .

When they surfaced tonight, he'd get a signal off to Dundee, repeated to Admiralty and Lerwick. Position, course, and speed: operation successful, and the names of the passengers on board: one U-boat sunk, date, time and position of the sinking: one A/S trawler sunk, date, time, position. And –

'Captain.' MacGregor looked up, startled out of his thoughts and plans. Bishop Dalen stood in front of him: around them, the men of the White watch were at their stations and Crawshaw, behind him and on the other side of the ladder, was fiddling with the trim. From up for'ard, a clatter of pans and dishes indicated that Ellis and the Chef were preparing for lunch.

Seeing the bishop's eyes, the set of his mouth, his hesitance, MacGregor knew at once what it was that he'd come to tell him. Over all the triumph, elation, rising to drown the sense of satisfaction and relief, a knowledge of enormous loss rose to choke him. He felt the grief in his eyes and he turned away, grasping the steel sides of the ladder, seeing nothing except that deep and gripping tide of sorrow: he rested his forehead on one of the thin, cold rungs, and he couldn't speak, or meet the bishop's eyes.

Dalen put one hand on his shoulder. 'He had no pain, Captain. He just stopped breathing. At the time of the last explosions, the distant ones . . . '

So there'd be more than signals, this evening, when *Setter* surfaced. There'd be a roll of sewn canvas, itself wrapped in a flag: it would be hauled up through the hatches into the bridge and the bishop would read from the book of Common Prayer, *Forasmuch as it hath pleased Almighty God of his great mercy to take unto himself the soul of our dear brother here departed: we therefore commit his body to the sea* . . .

MacGregor thought, blindly, *Brother.* Yes, it could be. It would be no worse, hurt no more if it was. The job was one of destruction, sinking, killing: but the mainspring of the matter was humanity. Not your hatred, but your love.

MacGregor turned and faced the bishop, a man whose eyes, in sadness, matched his own.

'Sir. The ladies of your party should use the wardroom now. Until this evening. It'll be crowded, but we can lunch in two sittings.'

'Of course.' The two of them moved for'ard together, to the wardroom and beyond. The subject of their discussion must have been obvious to the men on watch; none of them looked at each other, or at the Captain, or at Bishop Dalen. The 'planesmen watched their gauges and the bubble in the spirit-level: the helmsman watched the steering indicator, and the E.R.A. of the watch was checking over his panel of diving control instruments as if he was expecting to find something missing among the valves and levers. In the corner, the Asdic operator twiddled the knob on his set, his eyes on his own fingers as they worked it round, and the messenger was staring aft, through the doorway which led to the engine room. This was Watch Diving, daily routine, as *Setter* crept westward at periscope depth. Tonight, a hundred miles offshore, she'd turn south. Her diesels would rumble into life and drive her forward, thrusting powerfully through the waves and staining the sea astern with a broad track of white where gulls would drift and soar and scream their weird, sad cries: and *Setter* would drive on southward, towards the safety of the long, dark nights.

THE END